# BONA FIDE
# COWGIRL

## JANA DAHMEN

Cover Art – Jana Dahmen
Publishing Coordinator – Sharon Kizziah-Holmes

Paperback-Press
an imprint of A & S Publishing
A & S Holmes, Inc.

ISBN -13: 978-1-951772-01-7

# ACKNOWLEDGMENTS

To Karolyn Cleveland who encouraged my writing for twenty-three years. Even when I called her in the middle of the night, she encouraged me to continue.

Thank you to my sweet husband, Marv, for patience and love when my head is buried in a story and to my children, Tim, Megan and Malori who have always believed in me. I love you all.

I'd want to thank Terry McDermid for sponsoring writing retreats feeding my soul with energy that flows into my fingertips.

Sharon Kizziah-Holmes, at Paperback Press, has helped me as a friend, fellow author and a publisher. She is the catalyst I needed to birth my book. What a beautiful spirit she is!

I must thank my characters of the fiction realm who came to possess lives of their own. I miss their passions and sharing adventures with them every day.

# PROLOGUE

## *1878 New Mexico Territory*

Ruby Blake's eyes yawned wide open. Her body was paralyzed with the overload of sounds and images. Adrenaline pumped through her body like a snake's venom and triggered a rhythm of hammer-like pounding in her skull.

The bloody terror before her was more than a nine-year-old could ever begin to process accurately. She didn't want to witness the horror transpiring in the theater below her vantage point; yet, she was as powerless to turn away from it as a stone.

She shielded her baby brother's view like a mother hen in the folds of her skirt. As if possessed, she protected him from the devil's demons at work. Vice-like hands covered his tiny ears but there was no such relief for her senses as horrid smells filled her lungs with vile fumes. How could she explain such tragedy to him when she had no understanding herself? She had no experiences to interpret the cruel acts by the hands of these men! Little idea did she have that this shameless loss would haunt her all the days of her life.

Her heart pounded to near bursting in her chest and each beat physically hurt. Was it possible for it to quit beating altogether? She did not know. A fierce determination to save Bowie at any cost took precedence over the wicked devouring images of fire, torture, murder and waste below. Though she was shaking so hard her teeth rattled. Her brain filled with the piercing, unnerving, coyote-like sounds of the bandits and the screaming of her mother. She became aware that Bowie was no longer struggling against her.

She held Bowie's face firmly against her body to squelch any chance he might make a noise that could reveal their location. At first, he squirmed against being constrained but now he'd gone limp with the forced submission. The fear that she had suffocated him overwhelmed her.

She dared not move but relaxed her aching arms enough that she could feel him breathing. He was over-heated and sweaty but without a doubt he lived. Ruby needed to move him soon. Though she felt fairly confident the rise they stood on was well-camouflaged by the thick, scrub brush, she continued to stand like a statue.

Time seemed to move in slow motion as did the suffering of her mother. What seemed like forever was less than an hour. Just when Ruby was sure she could take it no longer, the noise stopped. The silence was deafening. It was finally over.

She stood in flaccid shock after the banditos road out and over a hill in the distance. Bowie's whimpering brought her back to the reality of the moment. Now what? The breeding stock was gone and the cozy home place and barn were in flames. Everything was blackened and already beginning to smolder in places. The gentle swinging of her pa, hanging in the tree by a rope threaded under his armpits, and the body of her ma sickened her and she retched. What should she do? What was she able to do?

Even if she covered the ears of her heart, she could still hear the shouted words of the Mexicans. Ruby could not understand the language but she recognized the sounds of evil. The constant, hysterical laughing and bantering still made her shudder. The crack of the shots splitting the air and riddling her father still made her cringe. The howls of the bad men had burned furrows into the very flesh of her young mind.

Only death, destruction and waste remained as black billows of smoke curled into the sky. How was it possible she could hear so much violence through the silence that remained? How could she still see so clearly the viciousness of the vaqueros after they were long gone? The blue sky and the soft, fluffy clouds were out of place.

Bowie, the young colt, and Ruby were all that survived. Nothing more of their world remained. These thoughts replayed over and over in Ruby's head. She did have the things her mother had packed for them in the sack. Little did her ma know these bread, butter and jam sandwiches would be the last meal she would ever prepare for her children.

Bowie renewed his struggle and the motion snapped Ruby out of the fog that engulfed her. Her knees buckled and took both of them to the ground. She panicked briefly, but the thought of the family's shelter in the rocks above calmed her. She had a clear course of action to follow now and she felt the urgent need to move as fast as possible.

Pa had taken the family there many times before. The excursions had always seemed like a romp and play time. Now the hidden place stood between her little band and death.

She had heard Pa tell Ma often to take her and Bowie there if there was a sign of trouble. Ruby figured that today's attack was the sort of trouble he meant. He said that they would be safe in the rocks. Ruby had heard everything Pa had stressed. The difference now was that Ma wasn't with them. Their sweet and beautiful Ma who sang to them lay below worse than dead and very much silent. The flames were licking her up.

Ruby was only able to move because she had to get her brother to the safety of the shelter. No tracks could be left that might be followed and she'd wipe them away the way Pa had taught her. She had no doubt that Bowie was now hers to protect with her life. Ruby felt the weight of the responsibility. She would be precise in following her parents' teachings and she would always be diligent.

She had to face the cold, hard facts that Pa wasn't coming for them and that this was no game. He was still swinging from the tree in what used to be the yard. He was riddled with bullets. No, he wouldn't be coming and she didn't have any more time to indulge in fears like a child.

*"Don't be afraid, Ruby Red. Get your wits about ya,"* she could almost hear Pa whispering.

*"I'm just a little girl, Papa, but I'll try to do everything I can to keep Bowie and me alive."*

*"That's a good girl, darlin'."*

Ma's screams and the following silence after the last man sliced her throat crept into her thoughts and drowned out the comforting voice of her pa. It was too much to stomach. A guttural sob came from deep in Ruby's throat. Salty tears as big as raindrops rolled down her cheeks. She wiped them away roughly with the back of her hand and willed herself to toughen up and cry no more.

She wouldn't do anything to let her parents down. She'd rise to the occasion and handle this mess. She had an important job to do as the head of her family. She would not let her little brother die. She'd never let him down! She would always keep him safe.

Heavy of heart, tired and scathed, Ruby squared her shoulders and gathered up the sack along with her brother's

4

soft little hand. The colt had roamed a distance away but she easily caught hold of the short lead rope tied around its neck. She turned her small party toward the shelter waiting for them higher up in the rocks. The shallow cave held water, hard tack, dried fruit, beans and jerky sealed in crocks. Blankets, a knife and a gun along with ammunition waited there too. She vowed she and her charges would make it together one way or the other.

# CHAPTER 1

## *1888 South Texas*

Ignoring the weathered gallows, Marcus Dobbs looked beyond them. He'd been watching a dust trail for some time in the distance. Now he could see the shapes of a horse and rider approaching from the south. He squinted bringing the wavering mirage into focus. It was insignificant and hardly worth tracking but there was nothing else to concentrate on and he was bored beyond tolerance. Judge Roy Bean's idea of a jail was three outdoor holding pens with none of the amenities of home. Between the cloud of dust being stirred up on the road, the sun and the distortion of a rider wavy in the heat, there was nothing else worth being curious about that was in any way positive.

This diversion was in sharp contrast to the crystal-clear view in the forefront of his line of vision. Two pine coffins had been unceremoniously delivered this morning. They now stood at attention on the saloon porch like proud soldiers on guard duty. He'd been trying hard to ignore their gaping mouths. They were there and ready to fill their bellies with rotting human flesh.

He had made a morbid game, which now bored him, of speculating which two prisoners in his cell might never see the light of day again when the nails were driven to close the lids forever. Not for one moment did he consider that was to be his fate. Still, being held by the notorious, irrational, hanging judge niggled at his nerves regardless of how hard he tried to ignore his situation.

Marcus had no idea what the prisoners' collective crimes were. None of them were inclined to talk except for the foul-mouthed trash squatting on his heels beside him. For some reason, this disgusting man seemed to think they were pals and he had attached himself to Marcus like a tick.

As for himself, Marcus had been hoodwinked into defending his right to pass on a public thoroughfare. He wasn't looking for trouble at the time and he'd never meant to fight. It was unfortunate that the challenger, who'd tried to keep him from passing, didn't cotton to getting his hat blown off, his cheek grazed and an ear notched during the fracas. The other man started it and naturally Marcus finished it but his friends apprehended him.

Marcus kept checking on the steady progress of the horse and rider making it closer to Langtry, Texas. The sight of a fair-haired girl on a magnificent mount caused him to gape slack-jawed at the pair. The fine stallion stepped regally and the young female rider held her seat easily. In fact, she straddled the huge stallion and commanded him much like a man. She was just as pretty as a picture dressed in men's buckskins. There was no way she could be mistaken for a man!

Curiously she was armed to the teeth with a set of serious side arms hung low on her womanly hips with a scabbard attached to either side of the saddle. She was armed with both a shotgun and a rifle. A big knife jutted out at the waistline. Whether or not she could use those weapons remained a question. She was asking for trouble. She appeared to be ready for action. Marcus doubted she could handle herself but maybe she was part of a wild west show. He'd seen one of those once. What this she-male did do, for sure, was to stir a fire in Marcus' nether region.

*What the hell?*

As the woman approached the saloon, he admired her form and confidence as well as her generous curves. He had a fondness for turquoise and the stones set in silver on her hat band danced in the sun. They looked out of place on the old worn hat. A profusion of straw-colored hair hung to her waist. She was intriguing to say the least.

*Oh Lord, what I wouldn't give to be her friend for an afternoon or two...maybe three!*

# CHAPTER 2

Ruby Red, as determined as ever, rode into Langtry on a mission. It was a business trip. She needed another hired hand to help wrangle the new mustangs she'd just run into one of her paddocks. Uncle John had advised her against taking them on top of the horses she already had to finish for delivery to the fort. Headstrong and stubborn as usual, she'd signed the additional, larger military contract. She didn't listen to his advice. She had need of one more man to make what she'd bitten off happen.

Uncle John would have one of his yelling fits if he suspected she was hell bent on recruiting an outlaw from Judge Roy Bean's jail. With a knowledge of most of the residents in the town, she didn't know a local man who suited her purposes.

She needed a tough, seasoned man with true grit, few vices and he couldn't be much of a desperado. He had to ride hard and rough and be able to work from sunup to sundown. Some experience with horses was necessary though she was willing to quick-train any man who showed to have more sense than a horse.

*Lord, I know that I come up with and act on ideas before I ask for your counsel. Forgive me, please. Now, if it's not too late I want to turn this over to You. I should have asked for Your help first but I have faith You will lead me to the right person.*

Finishing the prayer for guidance after the fact, Ruby rode in between the hanging platform and the saloon. She reined Big River to a halt in front of the Jersey Lily Saloon. Two freshly-constructed coffins stood straight-backed and upright in front of the establishment for affect. The lids stacked to one side of the porch emphasized that they were waiting to be filled with the remains of human beings. Imminent death was implied by their gaping emptiness. The shadow of the graying rope swayed in the gusty wind. It was a grim and ominous scene, indeed. The scare tactic made her feet feel itchy.

The relentless, gritty dust was blowing around her with a fierceness and it penetrated her hair and clothing. A tumble weed rolled and bounced aimlessly along. Being propelled by the never-ending West Texas wind, it loosely followed the dirt path that served as Langtry's Main Street. The journey was hindered by snags on this and that and it zigzagged from either side of the road bumping into obstacles that altered its course. It was a drunken drifter being tugged and pushed by an ocean of wind.

The features of Langtry, Texas were bleak and lonely. The amenities made for a difficult environment for living. It held little forgiveness and often fatal consequences that the innocent as well as the guilty were often exposed. It was a desolate and isolated place that the lawless often found themselves caught in. The quirky judgements of Judge Roy Bean ruled supreme here. Outlaws were incarcerated like flies getting caught in a spider's web.

She shook her head with the knowledge that Uncle Roy had a flair for theatrics and used this gift often to intimidate and bully his law throughout the territory. He reigned with an iron fist. She would be the first to declare that his methods were quite effective but that didn't make her agree with his strategies. She accepted his fear-tactics though and turned her back to his blatant cruelty most of the time. She did not care to visit Langtry often.

Outsiders to this desolate part of Texas didn't know that Judge Bean sentenced only the vilest and most dangerous criminals to the gallows as he often made it appear otherwise. He was a master at starting rumors to serve his own purposes.

He often fined the jailed for whatever was in their pockets and paroled them out to area farms for a stretch of back breaking work. His reputation as the Hanging Judge was a tool he used to control and repel outlaws from this territory. Bad men often made wide tracks around his domain. The word was to stay away from his harsh reign and his saloon court justice.

Set to the right side of the establishment in the sun were three metal-barred jail cages. There were no protective sides, floorings or coverings. It was just dirt and the hot sun today. There was nothing to sit upon or places to lie except for the hard ground. Regardless of the season, prisoners were held in the open air until the all-powerful judge took a notion to hold court.

Today seven poor souls squatted, stood or lay on the ground. An unpleasant odor emanated from the urine and body wastes that had been deposited at the back of the cages. The men were divided evenly between two of the pens, and a solitary, forlorn-looking woman lay on her back in the dirt of the third. Bloated flies buzzed around her beaten face. She was too pitiful to even swat at them, but her eyes were open and shielded from the sun by her grimy forearm.

Ruby ground tied Big River at the rail and stepped around the porch for a closer look at the filthy menagerie of people. She took a long, thoughtful perusal of the gallows and the ever-ready-nooses. What a menacing and threatening view designed to torment. It gave prisoners the full idea of the consequences. She turned back to the bird cages and studied the pickings before her. Most were a sorry, miserable lot of humanity who could not be trusted to empty the chamber pots in a brothel. Her quick perusal discouraged her.

The woman wearing a worn, faded, once-frilly red dress with torn, black stockings appeared to be ridden hard and put away wet. Her shoes were worn through on the soles in many places. Her face bore the effects of a recent beating with blood crusted around her swollen, snotty nose and chapped mouth. She was obviously ill and ailing.

Three of the men were filthy with weeks of crusted grime. They were either sick or had whiskey-pickled brains. Their blank faces showed no awareness of their dire circumstances. One was standing with intelligent expectation on his face. The other was lazily arising to lean suggestively against the bars by him. The lazy-looking man fisted his hands around the crossbars to steady himself. He sneered and snickered as she approached. A mumbled insult reached her ears but she chose not to react. The other man lifted the front of his hat in polite greeting, straightened himself to his full height and looked Ruby directly in the eyes with respect. He seemed out of place in the company of these dirty miscreants.

His eyes caught her attention and their gaze held. The handsome man had clear, alert and responsive brown eyes that sparkled like polished Mexican agates. He looked her over just as she studied him. She'd never been the kind of girl to try and impress a man, but she wondered if she met with his approval.

Surprised by her growing interest, she quickly discarded the thoughts and leaned toward a more analytical approach. This man was dressed well and much cleaner than most of the cowboys at the ranch. He was amazingly well-built and had an air of self-reliance and confidence that spoke before he opened his mouth. She respected that.

Walking closer to the two men leaning on the bars, she calculated their individual worth with an assessing eye. There was an extreme contrast. Finally, she spoke in a low, deliberating voice addressing both but focusing on who presented himself better.

"What experience do either of you have with horses? Have you ever broken free-range horses before? Have you worked on ranches?"

The man who had maintained eye contact throughout her scrutiny gave a hint of a smile. He touched the brim of his hat pushing it back slightly.

"Yes, ma'am! I've worked horses including wild, tame, raw, mean and gentle. I'm a seasoned wrangler. I've worked on three different spreads." Appreciation registered on his face as he looked at Big River again.

"That stallion you rode into town captured my eye from down the road a piece."

*I saw you too, little sweetheart.*

"Impressive lines with iron-strong confirmation topped off with a pleasing color and the size of a behemoth makes quite an impression on a man who knows horses. He's alert, holds his head with attitude and is one robust specimen of horseflesh. He was bred for speed and endurance. I'd venture a guess he's used to stud. Any rancher would be a fool not to build a reputation on him."

This cowboy had used the right words. He definitely had her attention now.

"Why are you in jail?"

"Oh, a lack of good judgment and a definite act of being shanghaied. I got into a little altercation just outside of town as I was riding in yesterday. Let's just say a man and I didn't agree upon who had the right-of-way. He didn't take kindly to having his hat hit the dirt and one ear pierced as a result of us talking it over. It turned out he worked for the judge in there. It was just my sorry luck. I wish I'd turned around now and gone a different direction."

Ruby nodded. She could easily believe that he was here on trumped-up charges. He'd been caught between Roy's short fuse and one of his braggarts who was trying to earn points with the judge. The enforcers he hired were more like criminals than law-abiding employees of the court.

Judge Roy Bean was the law west of the Pecos and not even the men at the capitol in Austin questioned his radical, unorthodox ways of managing this almost lawless part of Texas. They didn't care who he chose to work for him.

He and her uncle John were thick, old friends going way-back to childhood. He'd known her pa well too. Even her godly uncle looked the other way when it came to the judge because he remembered what the Rio Grande territory was like before his friend set up his circus court.

She sure as hell knew firsthand about the lawlessness reigning before Uncle Roy cleaned house. He ran most of the bandits, outlaws and rogue vaqueros out of his jurisdiction. He was the reason honest people can settle this place and raise families. She'd always love him for that.

Roy Bean had extreme quirks. He was notorious all over Texas for being unpredictable, reckless, inconsistent, drunken, volatile and cruel among other things. On the recommendation of the Texas Rangers, Austin gave him an unsupervised hand. His bizarre interpretations of the law bore results. That's all they cared about.

Ruby's spine stiffened as her body went into alert mode. The other man glared at her with hungry eyes. She frowned at his yellowed teeth and the dried tobacco juice streaking down his whiskery-stubbled chin. There was no sign of honor in his face. Ruby detested men like him.

"Horses are just like women, honey." He breathed the words out with a thickened tongue and horrible breath. "I know all about fillies and what they need to behave. I jerk a knot in their tails and they come to heel fast." His eyes ran insultingly from one end of her to the other. Her skin crawled with loathing.

"If you're hankering for experienced handling, then I'd fit you, darlin'. I think a hard ride would take the sass right out of you. My hands can be warm and gentle if you're nice or rough if you're not." His hardened eyes caused her to cringe as he raked them over her body one more time. Then he farted without a hint of humiliation.

"Do I look like a steak? Cut the dominant, vulgar talk. On second thought, don't say another thing. I detest filth like you!"

This uncouth, vile idiot had riled her too far with his impertinence, insinuated threats and unsolicited liberties. Just as fast as a rattler, one of her hands struck through the bars with a speed that took him off guard. She grabbed him by his dirty hair and slammed his forehead against the hard bars three times bringing blood and a rapidly rising knot. The bars rattled like thunder. Even the woman in another cell opened her eyes. The deep gash bled like a stuck hog and needed stitches but he'd have no luck getting them. If Uncle Roy heard about him insulting her, he'd hang.

The other man had instantly gone rigid and ready to defend her but with the other hand she'd drawn the big hunting knife equally as fast. She held it at eye-level to the addlebrained man while easily securing his injured head by a handful of his filthy hair. His pained reaction was audible, and he bellowed in surprise as he saw the blade of the knife glinting in the sun. He was trapped like a fish in a barrel.

"You call me Darlin' one more time, you call me Sweetheart, or you even think another untoward remark and you'll regret the day you were born. I'll carve your liver out and leave it to putrefy in the sun!" She banged his fingers loose from the bar with the bone butt of her knife. He stumbled backwards holding the shattered appendages of his gun hand. He retreated to a back corner to lick his wounds. The vile man cradled his injured hand mumbling obscenities and words of distress directed at no one in particular.

She dismissed him as one would a pesky fly. Looking totally unflappable she turned her attention to the other man. She picked up the conversation with him as if it had never been interrupted.

"What happened to your horse, cowboy?"

He was rendered momentarily speechless by what she'd just done but pointed toward the livery behind him. He was truly shocked by her command of self-defense. He'd seen many men over the years who wouldn't have handled themselves as well. While being a female in a man's world might be thought of as a handicap, it didn't seem to be one for this girl. The question of whether she could use her arsenal or not had just been answered. Her actions, speed, guff and skills told a story. He'd heard tales of able cowgirls but never met a bona fide one until now!

"Well, I'm assuming he's safe over at the livery. At least I'm hoping so. I haven't seen him since he was led inside. I'm in no position to expect a favor, ma'am, but could I ask you to check on him? I'd surely hate to lose a horse like Bob. He's been a good and faithful friend. I've led him into a muddle this time."

Without uttering a word, Ruby turned and walked the short distance to the livery. Knowing how frantic she'd be about Big River under similar circumstances, she'd not only see about him but would take him to the ranch instead of leaving him here. She could feel the man's eyes following her.

This man was different than the others she'd come across. She couldn't put her finger on what was making her insides queasy around him. This feeling he triggered was not sensible. He was nothing but one more cowboy! There were plenty like him at the ranch, but this man had an air of integrity about him that garnered her interest. A look into the condition of his horse, the contents of his saddle bags and an inspection of his tack would tell of the man's character and habits.

# CHAPTER 3

Marcus Dobbs studied the plump ripe peach of her backside as she walked away. She had admirable curves. The buckskins didn't hide the places he wanted to hold onto with his hands. She carried herself with the determination and purpose of someone in charge. How unusual to find in a woman! Marcus found her attitude alluring. He reminded himself to calm down. She was nothing to him. He should stop thinking about things that are none of his never mind!

He shook his head in an attempt to clear it of ignoble thoughts. Nothing of his current predicament had changed in any way. The two, gaping coffins were still standing and the ropes were still hanging. The scent the fresh pine lumber carried by the wind was not comforting. He had no way to get himself away from the threat of doom that was thick all around him. He was a fool to indulge thoughts about a pretty girl right now. Damn, but she was quite a girl though! She was one hell of a strong woman!

The fact that she booked no nonsense called to him like a siren. She moved with a straight back with her head held high and walked with a commanding purpose. Her low, thickened voice put him in mind of sensualities. Dang, if he didn't like the way she takes charge of corruption. She responded like a lightning bolt! How neatly she had put that lowlife in his place without warning. She had acted out of instinct with no hesitation. She stood her ground speaking loud and clear and never backed down. No sir, she was fearless!

This display of sand was unprecedented in Marcus's experiences with women. It was certainly the only way for one to survive among men. Delicate women like his Ma and sister didn't fare well left on their own. The least he wanted to know was who she is.

Her soiled, worn britches bore the tracks of hard work. The mismatched side arms spoke of business. There was doubt now that she could use them both. She'd proved that by pulling a skinning knife as if it wasn't the first time. That long, sharp blade had been handled with proficiency. It was as natural as an extension of her arm. She knew what she was doing.

The legs of her pants were tucked inside scuffed boots and the sound of the small, jingly spurs put him in mind of the tinkling of a music box. The notes rang with a tune that reached something deep inside Marcus that had lain dormant his whole life. What was happening to his good sense? He had to get his thinking back on solid ground.

The dusty, sweat-stained hat was an anomaly adorned with the leather band embellished with silver and turquoise. It was like a crown on her head with the golden hair well below her shoulders in various shades of yellow, red, brown and silver. Her exquisitely fine facial features didn't match the bravado of her spirit. White, straight teeth and rich, blue-gray eyes like gun metal had reflected good breeding. His curiosity was aroused. She was a confusing and exciting female who commandeered his full attention like no other miss ever had. It was too bad he was locked up in this iron cage or he'd try to get to know her.

# CHAPTER 4

Ruby found Marcus's horse in the last stall. The grizzled, old hostler had nodded his head in the general direction when she'd asked. The black gelding with intelligent eyes was stout and built for endurance. The horse appeared to be well-conditioned, well-fed, clean and shod. He welcomed her attention greeting her with a soft, snicker, a light toss of his head and a sweet nudge. The tack that was hanging on nails by the stall was worn but in good repair and condition.

Ruby went through the man's saddle bags and found an old, worn Bible with the name, Marcus Dobbs, 1870, scrawled in neat long-hand. Soap, shaving gear, toothbrush, a tin of tooth powder, a couple of grungy drying towels, rolled bandages, two extra shirts, socks and a change of drawers and pants were neatly stored. Work gloves were tucked in with typical trail-grub. A bag of peppermints was the only evidence of extravagance.

She pulled out a small stack of letters tied together with a frayed, yellow hair ribbon and read the one with the most recent postmark.

*Dear Brother,*

*We miss you sorely every day. Thank you for the money you last sent. Ma is no stronger but no weaker either. I am working as a seamstress in the dress shop and Jim works as the blacksmith's apprentice. He is learning to fix wagon wheels and shoe horses. He enjoys the work and the blacksmith says that he's good at it. He's learning a trade. We're getting by well enough and, yes, have plenty of food, clothes and adequate shelter. You needn't worry about any of us on that account. We have everything we need except to hear Ma laughing again. She seems to enjoy it when I read to her. The preacher lets me borrow books from him. He's been really good to us. The extra funds you send buy Ma's medicines and make life more tolerable for all of us. I have even been able to put back a little for a rainy day by sewing. We pray constantly that God is keeping you safe and well. We're alright so don't you worry none. With your help, we are making it fine.*

*Marcie*

Satisfied with what she read between the lines, she paid for the horse's board with a generous tip for the old man. After saddling him and tying the bedroll in place she walked the gelding back to the railing to stand by Big River. The two horses made snuffling noises as they became acquainted with each other. The cowboy watched his horse and the cowgirl. She never once looked his way but walked boldly through the bat-winged swinging doors of the saloon as if she belonged there. They flapped loudly as she passed.

He was sure glad to see Bob again but unsure of just what this audacious female had in mind. He couldn't defend his property and the horse was at her mercy. He figured Bob could fall into worse hands than hers even if she took him. When he got out of this scrape, he'd track Bob down and reclaim him.

On the other side of the swinging doors Ruby stood magnificently with fists on hips and feet spread apart widening her girth. It was quiet inside except for the sound of shuffling cards, raspy coughs and the rattling of pool balls. The backlighting of the sun through the doors framed her silhouette creating an impressive sight. The cave-like room was dark and dreary in comparison. It took a minute for her eyes to slowly adjust.

A few men lifted lazy heads in silence and others mumbled, "Hey, Miss Ruby." No one acted as if it was unusual to see her inside the saloon where only men entered. Judge Roy Bean stood at the polished bar and raised his glass to her in salute. He remained silent as she walked forward.

"Uncle Roy, it's a little early in the day to be drinking."

"Did you come here to preach, Ruby Red? It's too early for a sermon or too late for one but not for drinking."

"I can see that you have a quota of two today by the coffin count."

"Yep, Ruby, that's the plan. I can't fool you! I never have been able to and I couldn't trick your dear pa either," he said lazily and with lack of energy. He balanced the half-empty shot glass between his fingers with practiced ease.

"I want one of them."

"What, a coffin box? Are you getting ready to kill someone, Hon? I'm sure they are deserving of it but does your uncle know?"

Ignoring his attempted levity, she continued. "No, I need a man to work for me. I've got him picked out. He'll do for what I need. Where's Maria?"

"Why–are you always here trying to annoy me? Can't a man enjoy the first drink of the day in peace?

"She's in the back and will be glad to see you. She's feeling poorly again today. Go on and sit with her for a spell. It'll break the monotony and cheer her some. We can do our arguing later. I'll be thinking of some good wiles to get you to ride out of this town–preferably alone."

Ruby laughed tossing back at him, "You know your charming wiles never work with me. I'm not afraid of you and I always know what I want and am bound to get it."

As she walked into Judge Roy Bean's private living quarters without knocking, she heard him mumble, "Unfortunate, for me, Ruby, as always."

Maria sat on the sofa sipping cool lemonade and patting her neck with a damp cloth. Her swollen bosom was practically spilling over the top of the lavender lace dress with the scandalously-low bodice. Her friend's thick waist was bulging with the swell of advanced pregnancy. A sweet little boy played on the floor at her feet.

"Ahhhh, Ruby! The very sight of you is food for my weary soul," Maria greeted in her sweet Mexican accent. "This heat is melting me alive today and causing my feet to swell like riverboats."

As Maria continued to speak of trivial domestic matters, Ruby sat and slipped off one of the woman's slippers and began to massage the puffy foot. Relief and pleasure were reflected on the woman's gentle face.

"What brings you to Langtry today, my good friend? You haven't been here in a while."

"I'm running over with work–wild, headstrong mustangs and Uncle Roy is always running over with idle men. I need another hand–thought I'd see what's available in the bird cages today. I scoped the picks out before I came in to see you. I found one that suits me.

"I'm leaving a list of supplies at the mercantile to be

picked up later as well."

"Oh, Roy will have plenty to say about your picking out one of the outlaws, I'm sure! Ruby, you always give him indigestion, you know. You're the only one not afraid to disobey him. It causes much discord between him and your uncle."

"That it does. They need a little shaking up now and then.

"Hey, Juan, I brought you something!"

The little boy jumped up throwing his thin arms around Ruby's neck and hugging tightly. "What is it, Senorita?" he asked smiling.

She pulled a cherry whip and a small, brightly-painted toy soldier out of her pocket. "Will these do, Nino?"

"You bet they will! Gracias!"

Ruby patted Maria's second foot when she finished rubbing. She drained the glass of cool lemonade the housekeeper had brought to her and visited for a while longer.

"Goodbye and I promise to return soon."

She re-entered the saloon through the family's door carrying a large tin cup of the cool lemonade, a thick slice of fresh bread and a wet rag.

As usual the judge tried to bully her into changing her mind about taking one of the prisoners. He knew John would not be happy with him for letting her bail one out and for allowing her to her ride off with him. The least he could do was half-heartedly try to dissuade her before walking out to the cages.

Ruby, with her mind made up, was always tiresome, but in truth she amused the judge too. He admired her spunk. His friend, John, had his hands full with his orphaned niece. His old friend couldn't handle her either.

Ruby walked directly to the woman's cell and spoke, "Hey, Lady, brought you something to eat and drink. Here's a wet rag to clean your person."

The defeated woman lifted her head from the dirt pulling up to her hands and knees and then crawling to the bars. Ruby stooped and handed her the cup. She drank greedily, slurping the sweet, cool liquid that ran down her chin to her neck before collecting in her grimy cleavage. After handing her the bread and the wet rag, she turned back to the judge.

"Are you finished codling the prisoners?" he grumbled. "I swear you try my patience, Ruby. I don't know why you come to town other than just to torment me."

Now Marcus had a first name for her. Ruby seemed fitting considering those plump, red, rose-petal lips. He liked the sound of it. He listened closely as Judge Roy Bean continued talking to her.

"You wouldn't know how that man cowering in the back got bloody would you? No, of course you wouldn't or at least you'd never tell. I swear, Ruby! Don't come around here anymore or I'll demand John tan your hide.

"I'm assuming this is the one you've chosen," the judge sighed in resignation.

He looked at Marcus and said, "You're one lucky vagrant, you are. I might have hung you tomorrow except for this soft-hearted saint taking an interest in your strong back." He didn't add that Marcus was the only criminal he would have actually agreed to hand over to Ruby today under any circumstances. This cowboy seemed a decent sort and he'd intended to release him sooner or later anyway.

"Listen up to the court, Man! You are hereby sentenced to six months of hard labor under Ruby Blake's authority, direction and custody. If you do not work to her expectations, she will bring you back and I'll have you horse whipped. If you run away from her during your sentence, I will have you hunted down and shot in the leg. If you do her any harm you will be hung with a loose rope. It will cause great, prolonged suffering as you shuffle the tips of your boots on the platform for days until you collapse breathing your last breath of life.    Do you understand the conditions of your liberation?"

"Yes–yes, sir," Marcus answered.

# CHAPTER 5

He couldn't imagine the crazy judge would turn him over to this unconventional woman! It would be a long six months with that list of penalties dangling over him. Maybe he would be better off to refuse and wait to be hung. Marcus chose instead to be bound by law and the harsh consequences assigned by Bean if he should waver from the conditions. Sticking around in this town was no choice and he readily agreed to the unexpected parole. He was eager to ride out of Langtry, even under the custody of this unknown cowgirl.

He silently thanked the Lord he was being released. He was beholden to Him for rescuing his carcass from the iron cage and granting him another chance. He couldn't wait to get out from under lock and key and get away from this crooked place. Surely tomorrow would be better than today.

Being handed over to this Ruby person had to go easier than the other possible scenarios he had been imagining. This was a good development for both his Bob and him. If nothing else he'd get food, keep and work. Marcus had a hankering to discover more pieces to the puzzle defining this unusual lady and he had an idea an adventure awaited him. At least he could look forward to some entertainment.

As the iron door clanged shut behind Marcus and the key was turned in the lock sealing the other captives inside, Ruby handed the judge several coins and thanked him. She turned toward the horses without another word or a look back. Marcus dutifully followed and kept his mouth shut. They both gathered the reins of their horses, but not until he had affectionately reunited with Bob and properly apologized to him. It was a joyous reunion.

Ruby led her stallion down the street in the direction of the mercantile. Marcus took her cue and again followed. This would be his lot now for better or worse and he understood that she was in charge. He was hers for the next six months.

At the railing of the barber shop she threw him a coin. "Get a bath and a shave. I need you to look as pink and clean as a boy from Sunday school. Back at the ranch, there will be questions about where you came from and I don't intend to get into it tonight. I'll take care of my business at the mercantile. Anything you need while I'm there?"

"No, Ma'am but thank you kindly. I liked how you helped that pitiful woman back there. She needed comfort and you saw to her."

"First, don't call me Ma'am again. The name is Ruby Red Blake. That woman is a sad, lost soul and that was about all I could do to help her. Uncle Roy won't hurt her himself, but his men likely already have and will continue to use her hard.

"Second, is your name, Marcus Dobbs?"

"Yes, Ma'–am. I mean, Miss Ruby. I go by Marcus. How do you know my name?"

"Bob told me when I rifled through his saddle bags," she grinned.

The sudden sunshine of an unexpected smile punched him in the gut!

"Oh, well, that explains it. Bob has never been able to keep his mouth shut around the ladies. I should have guessed he'd flapped his lips. I guess you read my private correspondence then?"

"Only the first letter on the pile. By reading between the lines, it showed me your good character. I know that you believe in God, you have a family depending on you and you're honorable about responsibilities even when they're not convenient. You also are organized and take care of your horse and tack. I know that you wash, change your clothes and brush your teeth. That's all I need or want to know for now. I'll have to see if you're a decent wrangler."

"Yeah, I'm a good wrangler. I'm also the son of a preacher and was raised right. Thank you for getting me out of that cell. I need you to know that I'll pay back the money it cost you to save my neck."

She threw her head back and laughed. The sight and sound of it kicked him in the gut. The affect was a surprise. He wasn't sure why.

"You'll earn it! Don't worry! Just so you know I traded you for a donation to the orphan's fund. Uncle Roy isn't all bad! He donates the money he gets through court fines to the orphanage.

"You don't cause me any trouble and we'll just call it square. You'll be busy on the Triple B spread and your six months of sentence will go fast. You'll pay me back with honest work and then some. We'll just think of this as a business arrangement between the two of us."

While Marcus cleaned up Ruby turned in the ranch's order and grabbed a few personal items from the store. She also bought a couple of biscuit sandwiches wrapped in paper at the café across the street and stowed the purchases in her saddle bags. Then she went back in the saloon to collect her new hand's firearms.

When Marcus stepped out onto the wooden walkway she was surprised by how handsome and fresh the man looked after a bath and shave. His hair was still damp and he was scrubbed with the smell of lye soap wafting in the air around him. He was tall and ruggedly good-looking with black hair, a chiseled face and a strong jaw. Ruby didn't think much on men as a rule but this one was sure no chore to look at.

She handed him a biscuit stuffed with fried pork. Looking directly at him she said in a book-no-argument voice, "There are a few things to get straight before we ride out. I'm not looking to be friends with you. I don't like or trust men. I have personal reasons that I'll keep to myself so don't try to figure me out.

"I'll be keeping an eagle-eye on you around my family, stock, ranch and possessions. They're the only things dear to me. The only things I demand in a hand is high-quality work, honesty, loyalty and kindness.

"Just so you know up front, there are few men I can't out shoot, out knife, out ride or out rope so don't try me. Never underestimate me or take advantage of me because I'll hit back hard. We'll get along fine if you don't cross me. I know more about horses than most and I demand that things be done my way.

"Never forget that I won't hesitate to shoot a man. You're smart enough to know the judge wouldn't even ask me any questions. He wouldn't even ask where you're buried."

Huh—a threat and he had no doubt she could carry it out. She was a hard one—all grit, mouth and hailstones!

"Got it, Boss!" Marcus answered solemnly with no hint of a smartass attitude. He totally understood the heft of her warning.

"I'll follow your lead. You've done me a good turn and I won't cause you to regret it. Pardon me for saying this but you're the most direct female I've ever come across, but I'll take it."

Without acknowledging his comments, she sternly

cautioned, "When we get to the ranch don't share with anyone where I picked you up.

"Uncle Roy had his reasons for putting you on lockdown but I believe you're a good enough man. I wouldn't be taking a risk on you otherwise. Others at the ranch might not see things my way or be willing to give you a fair chance right off if they find out where you came from. They're unnecessarily protective of me which can be a nuisance. Keep your mouth shut about our arrangement. They may smell a rat but they won't question my judgement if facts aren't thrown in their faces.

"I honestly need your help breaking a herd of hard-headed, tough-backed mustangs. You claim to be an experienced wrangler and I'll soon find out how good you are.

"Never will I hesitate to haul you back to Langtry if I see a reason. The judge will treat you more harshly than before. He's ever bit as hard as he sounds."

She paused and waited for a response. Marcus just nodded his head and said, "I get it."

"On the Triple B my real uncle, John Blake, is the law. Judge Roy Bean is not actually my uncle. He's a close family friend and he knew my pa and Uncle John when they were boys. Sooner or later he will tell Uncle John how I came by you and hopefully by then you will have proven your worth and earned honor.

"The ranch foreman is Pete. He lives in the bunkhouse with the ranch hands. He answers to Uncle John directly. Do anything Uncle John or Pete tell you to do but make no mistake you're working for me in the stables. There I am always the one to answer. You'll bunk in the stables too. All of my hands sleep there so that the horses are never left alone. You will eat at the big bunkhouse, and Blue John, my stable foreman, will decide your schedule and introduce you around to the other hands. He answers to me as well and you dang sure better do as he tells you regardless. You might as well know now that he's an Apache` Indian. If you don't like Indians then keep your preferences to yourself. He's a good man and I'd trust him with my life. I won't tolerate him being disrespected. He's one man whom I call a true friend."

"Uh--yes, Ma'--am. I mean Miss Ruby. I don't have bad coup with Indians and showing due respect won't be a problem."

"Jess and Mary Jane work at the ranch house and supervise the grounds. Any time they speak to you, address them back like you would the king and the queen. I love them both dearly. They're same as my grandparents.

"My little brother, Bowie, will fall all over himself to get to know you. In fact, he'll make an outright pest of himself. Watch your step around him. He's impressionable and he has a tender heart. He thinks about things differently. I'd as soon slit any man's throat than to see him hurt or taken advantage of in any way.

"You'll see a lot of him because he's a good hand with horses. He is going to take a shine to you. I'm the one who's raised him. I'm his sister right enough but more like his ma since our parents died a long time ago.

"If you have any questions just ask as they come to you."

Marcus nodded keeping his mouth shut and his eyes on Ruby.

"Oh, one more thing--I run a fair and square business. If you work out, you'll be paid fair wages just like the other cowboys even though you're secretly being held here against your own free will. I don't need nor do I want slave labor."

Ruby signaled her big, beautiful stallion good naturedly causing him to rear up impressively high into the air on his hind legs. Once he touched back on the ground, they took off in a flash.

"Well, Bob, I guess we better start working on our

exits!"

The big man and his own powerful horse followed obligingly. A good run suited them both after being locked up in Langtry and forced to cool their heels. They had little trouble riding through Ruby's dust and catching up.

# CHAPTER 6

Marcus shook his head slowly. What was there about a sassy girl with more brass than tact? She was a contradiction. Women didn't usually act this way. This arrangement was going to test him. He'd be hard pressed to make it six months with her as a taskmaster!

The unexpected good news that he was to receive pay would enable him to keep sending money to his sister. That's all he really cared about. The facts that he could handle horses while having room and board made the thought of working for little Miss Bossy more palatable.

The stable foreman, Blue John, greeted the two as they road in. Marcus saw that he was much older than himself. Ruby failed to mention that the man was a half breed, not that Marcus cared. It was easy enough to feel esteem for anyone worth their salt.

The stable foreman spoke softly and sparingly. He assigned Marcus a bunk and a stall for Bob. He introduced him to the other stable hands and took him to the main bunkhouse to do the same.

The grub was far superior to any ranch food he'd ever

eaten. Marcus ate his fill trying to catch up for the scant vittles he'd had in the past few days. He was aware that the ranch foreman studied him carefully. Pete shook hands with him but didn't converse with him to any extent. He figured that would be forthcoming soon.

Bowie showed up at the stables bright and early the next morning with his big yellow dog, Whiskey. Marcus would soon learn the two were inseparable. Bowie was a stout, blonde youth with enthusiasm in excess and rapid-fire questions. He was curious about everything. It appeared he had a natural connection with horses and good instincts. He was encouraged by Ruby and Blue John.

Ruby's boy was most fascinated by the newcomer. He showed Marcus his bird nest collection displayed on narrow shelves in the stable, his horse, his knife and Whiskey's tricks. He chattered non-stop and Marcus soon realized that Bowie didn't wait around for many answers from anyone before he hurried to the next thing. Everyone, including the boy, worked hard.

Marcus began to marvel at Bowie's poetic and philosophical perspective on ordinary objects, animals, nature and people. He was strong-bodied, good-natured, hard-working and nice-looking. Being both smart and innocent, Bowie's observations of the world around him always gave Marcus things to ponder.

No wonder his sister, Blue John and Pete all warned him to go easy around Bowie. He was a rare tender spirit and fiercely worth protecting. It was easy to fall onto the Bowie band wagon!

Marcus's name had been added to the big slate on the wall with his list of duties in bold, chalked words. His responsibilities were directly related to the care and conditioning of the raw mustangs. He quickly showed his worth at being a seasoned wrangler. He immersed himself into a steady rhythm of productive work that soothed him.

Though he'd been leery at first of the real possibility

that Ruby and Blue John would overshadow his every move, second guess his methods and try his nerves, he quickly found that was not the case. His experience and skills were not only recognized but encouraged. Any requests and suggestions made by the two were smart, helpful and logical. In turn, they listened to his ideas.

It was amazing how hard Ruby worked right alongside her men and how astute she was to the temperaments of her horses. She recognized each head as an individual with its own personality. He actually learned a few things by following her lead. Thanks to God he had no doubt that he was exactly where he was supposed to be.

The horse stock wore a different brand than the other Triple B cattle. Marcus didn't question why there were two separate brands but he did wonder some about what that implied about the lay of the ranch. Branding the new mustangs was scheduled to happen before the ranch round-up and was kept unconnected from branding the cattle. For the cattle, everyone would be front and center for the staging. This would include most of Ruby's stable crew as well.

Marcus was well-honed from many years of ranching experiences. Pete counted on him to be an asset. He had blended in quickly with the other Triple B cowboys and an easy comradery was establishing among them. Marcus was always a non-threatening team player.

Spirits ran high the week the big round-up kicked off. Every available body worked long hours on the ranges to find pockets of stock camouflaged in brush, draws and canyons. It helped that these critters stayed close to the water sources. Some cowboys made camps farther out to keep gathered herds from scattering.

The cutting, branding and castrating got underway even as stock was continually brought in closer to ranch headquarters. The breeding stock and older steers were already fixed but calves had to endure the traumatic procedures. Burning brands into the flesh of the calves would leave angry marks and tender hides. That was unfortunate but definitely necessary for the future of the ranch. The brand identified them as Triple B property. Proof of ownership meant everything to a rancher.

Once the work began a rancorous, singed stench, wood smoke and thick dust laid heavily suspended in the air at nose level. It lingered in a choking haze. Stink and grime adhered to every living and non-living thing. The foul pollution invaded mouths and eyes of humans and animals alike. Poor guiltless babes who'd been born to this hellish fate bleated for mamas who were likewise bawling for them. It was a confusing racket seeming to lack rhythm or harmony which in itself formed a powerful chaotic pulsing.

The rough handling and hurt caused unavoidable stress. Pain was the consequence of burning to mark and the cutting to make steers added insult to injury. Overwrought mamas bellowed louder than all of them with the maternal distress of separation. It all worked together to sound an old, well-played and orchestrated mayhem of noises in a most disorganized score. Texas cowboys relished the dance and beasts and men never missed their cues and beats.

Not one day would differ from another until the foreman announced the work finished. The sessions started before daybreak and ended at dusk. The name of the resulting melody was Exhaustion!

# CHAPTER 7

B rother and sister had lived on this ranch with Uncle John since Ruby was nine-years-old and Bowie was three. She'd soaked up every skill needed to defend herself and family and to be an independent rancher in her own right. She'd taught Bowie how to take care of himself and the ranch when necessary. Someday all of this would belong to the two siblings and they'd be prepared. Ruby loved this way of life and never desired to marry. She couldn't foresee a time when she'd willingly put herself under the authority of any man.

Her head was in the moment most of the time and right now, she and Big River were cutting and roping with the cowboys. The two together were synchronized perfectly and known far and wide as the best in the territory.

Well, well, would you look at Mr. Dobbs go? Dang, if he wasn't keeping up with her! "We'll have to step it up, River!"

Ruby felt Marcus and Bob pushing them with their skills but she found the challenge exhilarating. It wasn't often she and her horse were pushed to this degree. The new man was a steady, capable roper with a well-trained cutting horse. Both were doing their jobs easily and moved as one. Ruby started out heading and Marcus was heeling but every so often they amiably switched off to stay fresh. It turned out that they were practically equal in proficiency at both tasks. Seasoned, impressive and confident in delivery came to Ruby's mind in assessing Marcus's skills.

A man of this caliber must have other skills besides horses and ranching. Everyone just assumed she knew nothing of the ways that went on between men and women. The truth was she knew plenty. Since becoming a woman, she'd deliberately disciplined herself to block out thoughts that strummed her hidden womanly places with uninvited feelings. Why is it, Marcus Dobbs threatened her resolve?

Ruby had to work at keeping her mind on the business at hand! He was a gifted wrangler and an invaluable hand. She had to leave it at that. She liberated him from a bad situation and that gave her the upper hand. It was a nuisance he was strong, virile, healthy and handsome! She enjoyed looking at him.

Working as an adept and entertaining roping team garnered the attention and admiration of the men. Ruby's and Marcus's performances were dance-like. They both knew the moves and the communication cues and it made the work like a game. The horses were dynamically responsive to their riders and uncannily predicted the movements of the stock again and again. Ruby could not help but enjoy the mutual comradery and this did nothing to firm-up her resolve to disengage from the man's charm.

Cowboy and cowgirl coupled movements by nodding, pointing, whistling, making eye contact, sending readable body language and giving occasional directions hollered in thick, gravelly syllables until Ruby's head swam.

Bob and Big River dipped and turned swiftly and sharply teased the picks relentlessly. The mounts played, knowing when to ease back to remove slack and when to step forward expediting the way to completion.

Ruby and Marcus smiled at each other from time to time and even laughed out loud together. Relying on a natural intuition of when to twist back and then thrust forward in perfect tempo, they perfected the act best satisfied through timing.

The ground crew worked quickly to keep out of the way but yet to keep up. After burning and cutting, each animal's wounds were smeared with a greasy dope to protect from dirt and ward off infections. The confused calves were then run back by cowboys on horses into the main herd. On and on the adrenaline-charged pace went with demonstrations of knowledge, speed, agility, strength and courage. The stiff lariat ropes were rewound just so after each throw and readied for the next flight through the air. Ruby reveled in her good fortune to do what she loved.

# CHAPTER 8

H e could easily watch the woman all day. It was obvious she had no idea how beautiful she was. Her smiles and laughter affected him. They stole his breath away. This attraction was killing him slowly!

Marcus observed Ruby doggedly as she continually encouraged her stallion with praises and endearments. How could he wish to be the damn horse! He wanted to know what she was saying to him. The horse was responding to it. He couldn't be jealous of a dang horse. What a fool he was being!

Ruby and Big River had a definite inseparable bond and Marcus admired that. He'd recognized their mutual dedication to each other when he'd first seen the two together. The horse weakened her show of bravado. Other tells of vulnerability sometimes caught his attention too. He noticed her awkwardness on occasions when they accidently touched. Ruby had a habit of ignoring his presence and trying not to smile at funny things he said.

These fleeting signs of inner turmoil made Marcus want to reach out and comfort her every time. The tall fence she'd erected around herself effectively kept him and everyone else at arms-length. All her actions were swift, direct and always business. She left no room for personal relationships except for family.

He suspected she noticed him more than she demonstrated. Lord help him, but he had the desire to know the real Ruby and what made her tick. Perhaps she'd been hurt. It stupefied him that he would probably kill any son of a bitch who hurt her.

His deep thoughts were brought to a halt by the relentless clanking of the dinner bell. It came as a surprise making him and others jump slightly. It reverberated loudly from the chuck wagon positioned upwind from the bedlam. The men yipped and yelled in unison, finishing up their last sets of the morning. The hooting and yipping was clearly a sign of rejoicing for the promised reprieve from hard, hot labor. Cowboys looked forward to breaks in the action with food, water and rest. They were like school children being let out for recess. With haste, the horses were unsaddled, brushed and hobbled to graze and relax. They'd earned a rest too.

Marcus kept an eye on Ruby's whereabouts. He made certain to get behind her in the chow line. One of the men passed between them with the bucket of mountain oysters harvested from the morning's labors. The cowboys would have the fried delicacies for tonight's traditional feast. He'd never developed too much of a taste for bulls' balls but he knew he'd have to eat enough to avoid being the brunt of off-colored ribbing.

Hot, sweaty and sticky like all the other hands, he watched as Ruby rotated her shoulders and massaged her throwing arm and shoulder.

"Your arm's stiffening up." There was the tone of teasing in his voice.

Not to be outdone, she countered, "You can't tell me that your muscles won't be screaming tonight! I'd have to put you down as a liar if you did. The truth is we'll both need the liniment.

"Blue John makes the best Indian concoction around these parts. He keeps plenty made up and the cowboys come from all around to buy it from him. He'll give you some if you ask."

"You're right–we'll all be hurtin' tonight. Thanks for the head's up on the liniment. I'll talk to him right after I get the nastiness of the day washed off."

The cowboys in line ahead of them were pouring dippers of water over their heads to cool off. Some of it sloshed onto the tempting shelf of Ruby's chest. The moistened fabric took on a thin quality Marcus was not gentleman enough to miss. He was discreet for sure, but he wasn't dead. The cold water not only caused her shirt to reveal too much but it caused one nipple to harden and pebble under the wet, translucent cloth.

How could one covered nipple be more titillating than two uncovered ones?

She couldn't dump dippers of water over her head the same as the boys for that exact reason.

That's another risky situation she exposed herself to by working around randy men. Why did he care? It seemed her loving uncle should be doing a better job of keeping her away from those cowboys!

Marcus did not want to consider what was causing his tetchy emotional state. He refused to dwell on the reasons.

Perspiration was running down her back and staining her shirt. He could only imagine the fortunate trickle that was pooling between her breasts. It would be sliding down and collecting at her belt.

*It's not right for a woman to sweat like a man in front of men!*

Totally baffled by ridiculous thoughts that shouldn't be any of his concern, he knew she had every right to be here on her land doing exactly as she pleased. This was her home.

Now what was she doin? Lord, have mercy!

She was shucking off her chaps. It made him dream about what it would be like if she shucked her pants too. He took his hat off and held it in such a way that it covered his pride.

*As if it isn't improper enough for her to run around dressed like a man, now she's putting on a show by peeling her chaps off! Dear Lord, please help the man who takes Ruby on to husband. Taming this wild filly might best be done with a strap!*

Marcus fought himself not to admire her grime streaked face. An average woman avoided getting dirty but she was no average woman. Somehow honest dirt looked natural on Ruby. She was no hot house posy. It was a trivial matter and didn't worry her at all.

*I like that she's a rancher battling the odds and hardships and being a real cowgirl. Yes sir, Ruby, you've earned the title fair and square.*

Marcus knew his thoughts were ridiculous. He'd been giving them like caresses and his boss wouldn't like it. They were secret invasions of her privacy. He had no right to continue them. The fact that he couldn't tolerate other cowboys around her should have been a warning bell. He was falling for her and he could not help it. Looking around the area he could find no one else ogling her. No one seemed to be paying her inappropriate attention except him. They must have given up on her a long time ago.

# CHAPTER 9

A disturbed, devious, pervert of a man who resembled a store clerk more than a cowpuncher waited unseen in a thick, tangled circle of low mesquite bushes. To say that he was a dishonorable degenerate in disguise wouldn't even scratch the surface in describing him. It was not surprising that no one ever paid any mind if he was missing from the group and never looked for him. No one really cared where he was or whether he got to the chow line. The other hands stayed away and avoided contact with him as much as possible. Had they even suspected the danger of his criminal insanity, he'd already be gone from their midst.

He had no friend and was ignored by the same jovial cowboys who enjoyed harmless pranks, laughing and having a good time with each other. They had no time to share or have compassion for the likes of him. They rarely spoke to him or even looked his way. After the first few had offered a hand of welcome in the beginning and been met with a cold shoulder the new hire had been left alone like a nonperson. He had fallen through the cracks. It left him free to spy and plot.

Pete mistakenly hired Jake James because no one else had been available at the time. He was the last hand taken on before Ruby hired her new wrangler, Marcus Dobbs, who'd turned out to be first-rate and would be asked to stay on permanently. In contrast, Jake was a slovenly worker and his disposition was sewing discord among the others. If left unchecked much longer it would lead to trouble. Someone would eventually blow sky high. He'd seen situations like this boil over before. The foreman regretted hiring the awkward man. He'd ploughed ahead even though he'd had a feeling in his gut that something was off. There had been pressure to add another hand before the round up and Pete had gotten careless.

Pete had been hearing the mumbled grumbling among the ranks and had singled out three of the older hands for talks. It was against the unwritten cowboy code not to be a snitch. Pete had waded through what each told him, reading between the lines and pieced the vague remarks together like a puzzle. He figured he now knew the burrs sticking under their saddles. The men clearly hated Jake for being a shirker, a liar, a suspected thief and an all-around bastard! He was a disappearing, escape artist and those stuck working with him ended up doing their job and his too. He would have be let go after round up.

If any one of the Triple B boys had an inkling of the nasty, sadistic things rolling around in Jake's skull concerning Miss Ruby the man wouldn't have made it to another sundown. The dark fantasies he visualized with her in them were beyond disrespect. They were deadly dangerous, crazy and abusive. They all loved her, Bowie, John Blake and the ranch. Any one of them would die defending her.

# CHAPTER 10

Pulling off the hat hugging her damp head for hours, Ruby crooked an arm to wipe sweat from her face. She reset the hat at an angle allowing the breeze access to her heated face. The snug fit had creased a halo along her forehead extending to encompass the circumference of her head. It was not attractive but an occupational hazard.

A cowboy's hat was a tool, not an adornment. It had to fit firmly enough to stay on the head under all conditions. If headgear flew off constantly while working it would be a nuisance but could also cause a harmful mistake while trying to struggle with it or retrieve it.

As the men filled battered tin plates and cups, they scattered out taking advantage of scant shade. They broke into amiable cliques made up of friends. The pleasing sounds of laugher and talk could be heard from every direction.

Uncle John came from ranch headquarters to eat dinner with his men during round up. He butted into line between his niece and Dobbs. His robust voice poked fun.

"Ruby, are you keeping these cowboys in line? That's

what I pay you for after all."

The one-arm-hug and smile the big man gave Ruby was the demonstrative salutation of a parent. She leaned into the man and returned it with pure adoration.

"Have you heard hide from Bowie and Whiskey today?"

Answering so anyone close could hear Ruby laughed a glorious sound. "Oh, Uncle John, you know these men are the best of the best. They don't need me to supervise. Pete does such a fine job ramrodding these yahoos and they work so hard I mostly nap in the shade. Besides, I always learn tricks from these old boys. I don't teach them."

"Well said and very gracious, darlin' Miss Ruby," someone shouted in Texas twang. The cowboys still around the chuck wagon made various noises of agreement and approval.

"Bowie and his yellow dog rode in with the first wave of stragglers today. They were both in good spirits and raring to get back to hunt for more head. You missed them but they'll be home tonight. They were both dirty and tired," his sister reported.

Most ate quickly and retired in shades for a quick snooze. They used their saddles as back and head rests. With hats blocking faces from the sun, a few snores could soon be heard here and there. The call-to-arms would sound soon enough.

One cowboy was using his time to write a letter. It was probably to a sweetheart or his mama. A sad, soothing sound of a well-played harmonica could be heard from a distance. Cards were being played and tales were being told. Time was being passed pleasantly.

Ruby carried her plate and cup past small groups of cowboys to reach a quieter stand of mesquite trees. Marcus had not been encouraged but followed along anyway. He wanted to know more about this girl. He liked to talk with her about anything just to hear her voice and ideas. She rarely released personal information about her life and he always had to read between the lines. They mostly talked about ranching when Marcus could get her to talk at all. He was creative in finding ways to draw her out.

Without turning around she said, "Marcus, you need to eat with the other men."

He was not insulted by her cold suggestion. He'd already expected her dismissal was coming. Her indifferent tone fueled him to dig his heels in deeper.

"Forgive me for my continued perseverance, Miss Ruby, but I was thinking this might be a good time to talk. Give you a chance to tell me what you really think for a change. We could talk about the weather, the branding, green mustangs or why you never want to talk to me. You get to choose the topic."

Her last few steps quickened but he still followed not backing up an inch. They both settled to sit on a grassy spot side by side but not touching. The silence between them roared as they tucked into the grub.

Surprisingly, she spoke first. "You're good at cutting and roping. We did fine together this morning. If you're still here when it's time for rodeo we might enter as a team. Strictly we'd be representing this spread of course."

"Of course," he casually answered without giving away his shock. "It wouldn't be anything else. We'd ride for the brand. Our horses do most of the work anyway. No one would even notice us being a team."

"Bob has shown to have good stamina. Big River loves round-up time and always pushes hard."

This line of talk led to more general observations about the two horses and soon the conversation was flowing more easily. Marcus had hoped this might develop into a real conversation. They began to smile and laugh together about the many little things that had come up during the morning. They began to enjoy the food and just shooting the breeze. It would have seemed totally generic to anyone overhearing them but to Marcus it was huge.

They'd worked up appetites and sat silently off and on concentrating on the red beans, chunks of chipped beef and sopping up rich gravy with fluffy biscuits.

Ruby finally acknowledged, "Marcus, you're doing a remarkable job with the mustangs. We're advancing them farther and faster than I thought would happen. I was concerned I might have bitten off more than I could chew. I was edgy about spreading myself so thin that the contract would not be met on time. You are making the difference between success and failure. For that, I want to thank you generously.

"Look for a bonus when this is finished. Uncle John fought me on this contract. It's a matter of personal pride now to make sure I succeed. You're a talented wrangler. Actually, you have the gift."

"I told you in Langtry I could do what you needed but you couldn't have known that I was being truthful. You took a gamble on me that day and got me out of the crack where my tail was caught. I will always be thankful you took a chance on me. I don't mind telling you that I was worried. You don't owe me anything."

Ruby spoke with a voice full of gentleness. "Well, I'm just glad it's all worked out for both of us. Uncle Roy wouldn't have hung you but he can make things unnecessarily hard. You can count on that bonus, Cowboy!"

Jake James wasn't the only one interested in the duo. John Blake was watching his niece smiling & laughing from the chuck wagon. His big frame leaned against it with his legs spread and feet anchored for balance. One arm crossed over his body supporting his other elbow. His hand was stroking his chin deep in thought as he considered

Ruby with this new fellow.

"Well I'll be! I'd never believe it if I wasn't seeing it with my own eyes!"

"Yeah, they've been circling around each other for a while now," said Cook looking at the two. "It's harmless enough."

"Let's hope not too harmless, Cook. It's about time that girl enjoyed some courting and shenanigans. I was beginning to wonder if she'd ever discover the joy of being admired and loved by a good man who could handle her. I won't live forever. This is the best news I've had in a month of Sundays! I'd hurry them along if I could figure out how."

"Yeah–seems like I faintly recall a time when a few shenanigans were a lot of fun!" Cook chuckled as he turned back to his work.

Ruby had resisted all previous attempts by John Blake to pick out a suitable husband for her. Maybe she'd finally picked out a beau on her own. Evidently this relationship held promise if his eyes weren't deceiving him. John was delightfully surprised that Ruby Red was giving him a chance. They both were smiling and laughing.

Never before had she let any man into the stronghold that she'd locked herself into long ago. He was very happy to see her having a good time and enjoying a man's company. He'd make it a point to question Pete about him. If he passed muster John would get acquainted with him and encourage the relationship with his niece.

Marcus and Ruby were unaware that their association was garnering so much attention. Ruby's uncle was being curious out of love and interest, but a dangerous psychopath watched for catastrophic reasons. One spectator was good and the other was evil. The couple had no reason to suspect that trouble was blowing on the wind. A catastrophe of far reaching repercussions was about to change lives forever. Later, in hindsight, no clues of imminent danger would be recalled.

Pure wickedness had dogged Ruby without her knowing it for weeks. When Dobbs had suddenly shown up out of nowhere, his presence had fanned the flame into a wildfire. Once Marcus had been singled out as sniffing around the monster's prey a rage fueled by green-eyed jealousy released the demon with a roar. A possessed mind can spawn lascivious thoughts, sick plans and violent actions and devastation is always a foregone conclusion.

# CHAPTER 11

Marcus spoke after both of their plates had been sopped clean and oatmeal cookie cakes were in hand. "Now I need a nap," he laughed rubbing his shoulder as if in pain.

"Don't get lazy, Cowboy! We'll be saddling back up soon. Our horses will probably run off when they see us coming."

"Naah! I doubt that. They're probably saddling themselves as we speak. They like this work more than we do! Those two aren't the average run of the mill horses. We're riding some prime horse flesh. Big River is the stuff of legends, Miss Ruby."

"You like my horse?"

"Of course I like your horse! Around you he's a pet and a mighty pesky one, but on the job he's all business and knows what he's doing. He doesn't like anyone else to mess with him but you. I have a hard time telling if you own him or he owns you.

"Other things stand out to me like his superior size, powerful conformation, his strength, intelligence and proud stance. Where did he come from? He's a finely bred, valuable horse and I don't think you happened on him by chance. It's a privilege to watch him when he's turned out. You sit on him like a queen. I've only dreamed of a horse as grand as him!"

Undeniable pride settled on Ruby's face. She liked the words Marcus had spoken and that he admired Big River. It was common ground where they could meet. This horse was her sun, and the moon and her comrade in arms.

"He's more than my horse. Big River is my past–my history. He is a living, tangible extension of my heritage. He's a prime remnant of Pa's hopes and dreams that still live. He's quite literally the first valuable colt born under the Circle B brand. That's where Bowie and I were born too. All the horses on this ranch carry the brand. My heart is branded with it too! I'm keeping my roots alive and carrying on my pa's work with the help of Big River.

"Big River and I have depended on each other through the worst times. That makes him my solid rock companion. We've grown up together more on this ranch than away from it. We both started out together on the Circle B spread but staying there became impossible.

When Uncle John came to get Bowie and me, I was so attached to the colt that he brought him along with us. It was after–mmm…"

With more left to be said she paused. After a time of staring at the horizon she inhaled a deep, unsteady breath. It sounded painful when it was expelled. She never returned to the splintered thoughts.

"He's certainly no colt now. Big River has the power and he gives me all he's got every time I ask. His size is immense but it's his truly big heart that makes him so valuable to me. We've seen and learned a lot of hard lessons together through tragedies and fun times too. I am ashamed to admit he does have some awfully bad habits that I've encouraged. That's the way it is when a young child and colt cling to each other for survival and grow up together.

"I know you and everyone else think I've ruined him. That may be true but he's my horse. I've spoiled him just the way I like him so it's no one's business. He's definitely my pet and loyal as a dog. He's even saved my hide a few times. We both adore each other and he seems to understand this," she smiled.

"I refused let him be gelded. I knew Pa would never have agreed to emasculate him. I told Uncle John so when I was a little girl though I'm sure I worded it differently. It just made me sick to think of the possibility. I went childishly hysterical to get my own way. Uncle John argued that Pa wouldn't have wanted his daughter ripping around on the dangerous stallion he'd likely grow to be. My uncle was insistent that I'd get hurt.

"The conflict caused quite a stir around the ranch. Sides were taken and bets were made on who would win," she laughed at the memory.

"Obviously, I wore poor, sweet Uncle down in the end. Big River will never have any idea how close he came to the knife. It's important I saved him for breeding. Many excellent throws have come from his bloodline. Pa's dreams still have legs after all this time. Big River is an invaluable stud. He has a reputation for supplying good horseflesh and some of his offspring are doing the same. A lot of money from his willingness with the ladies has generated a wealth of horseflesh."

Ruby averted her eyes and was suddenly uncomfortable that she'd shared so much but she saw sincerity in Marcus's eyes. It confused her.

"I imagine you find me direct and unseemly for a woman, but I'm a rancher first. Raising and training horses suits me and I don't apologize for the indiscretions of the job." Her chin lifted in a challenge. She was on the defensive from a challenge that wasn't in Marcus's stare.

"In truth, I'm enthralled by your straightforwardness. It

shows confidence in your skills as a rancher and in your right to be just that in a man's world. Don't go puttin' words in my mouth that aren't mine, Ruby.

"Believe me, I understand how you feel. This is all I've ever wanted to do too. I'd never forfeit my right or try to take yours away. I think we both must have been predestined to do what we were surely born to do. I do reckon, Miss Ruby, we are of the same mind on that."

"Yes, well, I'm sorry. I shouldn't have been on the defensive. I'm just so used to having to defend myself. I've fought for so long to be respected in this business. I've had to work harder than a man to hold my own when everything is working against me. The constant struggle is tiresome."

"Tell me one more thing I'm curious about. What forged the relationship between the young girl and the horse?"

"Big River chose me when I was about eight. He was still suckling his mama. Unavoidable circumstances further bonded us together. As far as I know, he's the only one saved from Pa's original efforts." She paused looking off again. She had a sadness etched on her face.

"Pa was an intuitive horse breeder. He instinctively knew the combination of traits to breed together to eventually produce strength, size, color, intelligence and temperament. Big River is the proof of his success. All of his breeding stock was stolen but fortuitously I saved Big River.

Regret and grief salted her recollections and for a moment she looked younger than her years. The vulnerability showing on her face struck a blow to Marcus's heart as fierce as a kick to the chest.

"I called him Little Horse and Pa didn't correct me. After the two of us and Bowie landed on the Triple B, the hands started calling him Ruby Red's Horse. After he was strong enough to carry me, we took to running up and down the Rio Grande like a couple of renegades," she laughed.

"He got his forever name, Big River!" She smiled remembering her rashness. "Poor Uncle John was forever tearing his hair out from fear I'd injure myself. He finally put his hand to me in desperation. After a couple of unpleasant sessions over his knee, squalling and yelling to high heavens, he abandoned the idea. I was determined to bear his smacks stoically but I couldn't keep the unfairness and fury I felt silent. I was a trial!

"He finally gave me over to Blue John charging him to supervise my activities. I was willing to allow the kind Indian to keep track of me because he didn't keep me on a leash. He never tried to corral me but gave me attention and guidance instead.

"I think he liked the idea of running free as much as I did. Sometimes, I trailed him as much as he followed me! That man taught me so much about the land, the animals, the seasons, tracking, self-defense and being a real cowboy.

"Anyway, Uncle John named Big River without realizing it. Before Blue John took me as his duty, Uncle John would bellow, "Ruby, I told you to stay away from the big river!

"The name, Big River, just stuck. Whenever he couldn't find me he'd rant and rave about the big river. Someone, usually Blue John before he was assigned to shadow me full-time, would be sent to round me up. The ranch hands started associating the big river with my horse. Soon it became the common opinion that Big River and that girl were pains in the neck! Some still think that, no doubt.

"It's funny but I can't even remember breaking him to ride. He was totally willing to carry me as soon as he was physically able. Little girls typically played with dolls. I favored one big horse."

With that Ruby came to the end of reminiscing and stood with empty plate and cup in hand. She apologized, "Sorry, I didn't mean to go on so. I don't know what got into me. It's not like me to blabber so much. You probably got tired of listening."


He didn't think she'd even scratched the varnish of her experiences. He'd never known of a girl who preferred to work outside with loud, dirty men doing hard, physical work. She ought to be learning to bake pies.

Ruby heated his blood. She was interesting and he craved her company. He'd not experienced this level of excitement before around a woman. It made him careless and he was leery of the affect she had on him. She was so independent, bossy, and sassy that he couldn't imagine why he cared but his feelings had a life of their own. Ruby Blake had a commanding spirit.

# CHAPTER 12

The rugged, unforgiving Texas land along the Rio Grande was Ruby's element. It was all mesquites, cactus, thorns, wild hogs, rattlesnakes, scorpions and uneven ground. The wind seemed to blow from every direction all at once. The winters were raw and the sun and droughts were even worse. A natural drama played between the topography and the weather. It served up exciting variances as well as exasperating hardships for man and beast to live through. A single choice could sometimes mean the difference between life and death. It had always held her complete attention before Marcus arrived on the scene. He threw her world off-kilter.

*Damn him for coming to this part of Texas! Damn me for bringing him to the ranch. I hate swimming in muddy water!*

Thoughts weren't so crystal clear for Ruby anymore.

*I enjoy being around him too much. Double damn his sorry hide! What has happened to my straight thinkin'? Ruby–back off–now!*

Living along the Rio Grande had afforded her the curtain she needed for isolating herself. Solitude was what she thought she wanted but that was not so clear anymore. Today, she wasn't so certain. She couldn't quite make the 2 halves of her tattered curtain meet in the middle any longer. *Is this as good as my life gets? Is being alone enough for me? Dad-gum-it, I have half a notion to haul Marcus right back to Uncle Roy! I should beg the judge to hang him!*

Ruby had come to one of life's many crossroads and she had no idea which way to turn. Confusion filled her head in the midst of reason. On one hand, she could put off making a decision. On the other hand, she didn't want to miss out on anything. Ruby's center of gravity wobbled. She could feel herself toppling.

She had been so sure that men were off limits. Of course, she knew that wasn't true of her pa or Uncle John. They were the exceptions but maybe she'd overlooked some others as well. After all, Jess, Blue John and Pete were square shooters.

There were still the vivid memories to support that men were cruel. Men were shallow too. They easily sold their souls for easy women, drink, money and violence. It was always baffling to Ruby that so many women were eager to be used by them.

She'd long ago come to the conclusion that she would never turn the reins over to any man. She trusted herself and no one else to keep Bowie and her pa's dreams alive and safe. Curiously, it was vexingly tempting to explore being desired by this particular cowboy.

Ruby had built a persona on hard work and self-reliance. She'd honed muscles, deadly survival defenses and quick reflexes to back them up. She'd devised a way to supersede feminine weaknesses. She'd prepared herself to live a full life on her own terms.

Being a conscientious guardian, Uncle John had insisted that she know how to be cordial, polite and well-attired. She had mastered the rudiments of homemaking in order to please him. She knew and could perform all fundamentals expected by polite society and she had been educated. In her opinion, the contrast between what she considered important and the attributes feminine convention required were far apart. She found the latter to be trivial, time-wasting and not in the least challenging.

She chose physical work above needlepoint and went to bed each night so exhausted that she didn't have the energy to dwell on the right or wrong of it. This course she traveled was enough but Marcus scratched the shell of her contentment. He fanned embers that she didn't even know smoldered. Flames were beginning to lick at her.

*Marcus Dobbs, you've become an itch on my backside. I don't have time for this! I don't need you!*

Round up was an especially hectic time and now preparations were already being made to get cattle to market. The mustangs needed attention but only a skeleton crew had been left to work the stables. If she had enough surplus energy to waste thinking on daydreaming about a man, then she'd be wise to keep her mind only on the priorities that mattered and work that much harder.

The cowboys were cleaning up the area from the last afternoon of work. The chuck wagon had headed back to ranch headquarters. The worn out, filthy cowboys were starting to ride back free at last to relax. They each chose their own paces riding alone or breaking up into twos and threes to jaw. Some of them stopped and waited by the tank politely for her to pass. They waited to bathe as soon as she was out of sight. Ruby rode alone envious of freedoms men took for granted.

She hadn't expected Marcus to ride up beside her when the last day was over. Instead, she figured him to join the others glorying in the water. Her heart quickened when he reined in Bob to match steps with Big River. Her body went rigid with tension.

Without looking at him she spoke the speech she had been planning to make. She planned to talk to Marcus straight out.

"Marcus, your company during the hard days of round up have been pleasant but I don't need it anymore. It's time to fall back to our original boundaries. You're a ranch hand and on parole at that. I'm your employer and you're in my custody for the remainder of the six months you were sentenced. Let's keep this strictly business from here on out."

This girl always said the most amusing things. "That's a little harsh I think. I thought we've been getting along real fine."

She looked at him flummoxed by his refusal to just accept what she'd said. She kept her expression neutral except for one raised eyebrow.

"Surely you've noticed that I'm not afraid of speaking up. I'm asking–no– I'm telling you to quit making me a target for your company. In the future just do your assigned jobs–you're good at what you do. Respect me. Be content and accept that the relaxed atmosphere of round up is over for now.

"Huh! Well, I'll swan! Here I thought we'd gotten' acquainted with each other. To put it bluntly, I'm a man if you hadn't noticed and you're a woman which I have noticed. It's pleasant to pass time together. What are you afraid of? It can't be me. I've been trying to figure it out–got to be somethin' bad dogging you.

"From what I can figure it must have been painful. It doesn't have anything to do with me, Ruby! Let it go. Let me help you heal from it and move on. I'll listen to whatever it is that's eatin' you from the inside out. Level with me."

"Mr. Dobbs, you know nothing about me, and you won't

so quit your figuring. Stop it, now! The only thing I need from you is to do your job. Henceforth, I expect you to keep your mind on your work. Pay no attention to me unless the job requires it. There's enough at hand that needs your focus. That's what you get paid for on this ranch!"

With that dressing-down, Ruby Red kicked Big River into a faster gait and hurried ahead. She suspected the matter had not been settled. Marcus was proving to be as strong-willed and persistent as herself. Where Ruby had always had functional but distant working relationships with the ranch cowboys, Marcus had crossed over the line and this had turned into a situation that was not so simple.

She could feel them being drawn together and she felt frightened. No one had ever like-liked her before. The pressure of being possessed was too much to bear. Marcus crowded her personal space causing her to feel self-conscious and concerned about her looks. With him she had unfamiliar moments of feeling like a typical female. She'd understood standing on the sidelines, but she didn't understand one thing about this.

What in the hell was happening? She felt inklings for this man and couldn't think straight. Marcus was ruining her life! She made up her mind to close the gate on him! Ruby thrived on the ranch and enjoyed seeing after her baby brother and loved her horse. Uncle John offered just enough family for them and gave her freedom for the most part. Nobody bothered her. It was all enough.

She was always packing and ready for a fight. Blue John had taught her the art of hand-to-hand combat with larger opponents. She was not easy pickings. She didn't hesitate to do whatever it took. Big River and she made a formidable team in action.

No, she had no reason to feel threatened, but lately,

she'd had the prickly feeling that unfriendly eyes followed her. She couldn't get a handle on the creepy sensation that made the hair on her neck stand up. She just felt an intuition that trouble was coming but could never put a finger on the cause. She would happily take the bull by the horns and charge head on into trouble, but she had to see the bull's eye first. She would seek the counsel of Uncle John and Jess except that she had nothing to tell them.

Unfortunately, there was a cancerous menace lurking undetected under a dark cloud of evil that was building. The devil moved about his prey without raising any alarms and fed on himself. He was so crafty and illusive that he had visual access to Ruby most of the time. He hid behind an invisible identity he'd created for himself.

# CHAPTER 13

Marcus watched Ruby's back as she rode away. She was such a sassy spit fire! It amused him that she thought she could just ride away as if he couldn't catch her. Inspecting her perfect, ample peach slapping the saddle with the pounding of the rougher gait made the front of his pants fit more tightly. Her hair, shiny as the sun, spilled down her shoulders and further distended his desire. She was full of spirit and ripe for the taking. He wanted to take a bite out of her. Maybe she had met her match and didn't know it. She'd better keep an eye on him, or she'd be the recipient of a good, hard kissing.

Finding her both intriguing and maddening at the same time, Ruby's strong personality drew his notice. She was driven by a wildness that was as unstoppable as the wind. He could feel her intensity and observe her in her element, but he couldn't quite catch her. She was a squall with gusts and crackles of thunder and white strikes of lightning.

Marcus knew for certain that he couldn't sway Ruby with things that made ordinary young ladies giddy and malleable under a man's touch. She would never bloom like a flower with soft words. He'd sparked shallow simpering females who batted their eyes. The kind who needed constant care and supervision from males. A cowgirl like Ruby could take care of herself! She didn't flirt and pretend to be defenseless. She was a formidable challenger.

*Ruby, you're a bona fide cowgirl–a one of a kind–but you need to be loved by a real man. You're too big for your britches–ah, hell–you've done split 'em! You need an attitude adjustment–not too much–just enough to get your ornery attention. How about a trip over my knee for a few swats–might do the trick, Miss Ruby!*

Other men might back off under the challenge she presented but that never entered his mind. Marcus decided to bide his time until an opportune situation to confront her presented itself. In the meantime, he'd try to flush her out of his system, but he knew he'd have to address the problem directly.

Marcus wasn't the only one mulling over things. Ruby had restless thoughts of her own. Dobbs had weaseled himself into her head where he didn't belong, and she wasn't welcoming the idea. She tried to ignore, discourage and stay away from him. Now, she needed to outmaneuver him once and for all to dismiss him from her mind.

Dog-gone-it! Her eyes had taken over her brains! She always looked to see what he was doing. The handsome and virile cowboy never lost her fascination and she'd never get her fill. Ruby even noticed how well Marcus filled out his britches. She wanted to hate him with all her heart if that was possible. Instead, he made her feel flutters!

She watched as he was laughing and talking with the bunkhouse boys. They were drawn to him too. Even the other hands were drawn to him. Why did he have to be so likable? Why did his assertiveness and directness appeal to her? Why did he have to be so good with Bowie and Whiskey? *I want you to go away–disappear! I won't even tell Uncle Roy you're gone.*

*You dare to come in here treatin' me like a woman and an equal! Double darn you–you're not welcome!*

Childish jealousy jabbed her like a wood splinter. The way Bowie hung onto Marcus was irritating, but why wouldn't he when the man was kind and patient with him? Bowie quoted him constantly like Marcus was the authority on all matters. Ruby had always held that special place in her little brother's heart.

In contrast to the envy, Ruby also felt gratitude for the special attention Marcus lavished upon her brother. She did not plan to interfere with their friendship.

# CHAPTER 14

The ranch was buzzing with all hands getting the ranch headquarters ready for the annual celebration ending the round up. High spirits hummed all around the place. Spring cleaning was being done in every nook and cranny outside and inside. Nobody got out of helping with something. Ruby was in the house a lot more than she wanted to be baking with Mary Jane. At least it gave her a reprieve from constantly running into Marcus Dobbs.

Benches were set up for a church meeting. Construction of the plank tables that would hold the spread for the big pot luck dinner were being noisily set up. Neighbors and their hired hands would be dancing up a storm in the party hall. A social of any kind was an enticement in the area since Langtry was notorious for its volatile atmosphere. Good women did not socialize there. Men only took their families to the mercantile and the café briefly and the women were never unchaperoned.

Marcus was sticking strictly to business, as Ruby demanded, and she missed him making a nuisance of himself with talk. Instead, he had taken to the disquieting habit of studying her from afar. She tried not to look but was as curious as a cat. She could no more keep from peeking than keeping her tongue out of the socket of a missing tooth.

*I can't keep having it both ways. I can't keep enjoying his attentions and not wanting his attentions at the same time. I'm pathetic–all kinds of a fool!*

When caught looking back to see if he was looking back to see, she'd squint her eyes and frown working harder at her task. Sometimes Marcus smiled, tipped his hat to her and walked away whistling.

*He's making fun of me. I think I'll accidently-on-purpose shoot him in the foot and then act all innocent like. I'll just walk away whistling–that's what I'll do!*

She hated how he riled her without saying a word.

*He's got some nerve that cowboy has!*

Feeling flustered was foreign to Ruby. She embarrassed herself by allowing Marcus to so easily penetrate the wall of solitude she'd built. Under his scrutiny she had ten thumbs and no fingers. It was vexing and irrational to put that much store in his opinion. He made her weak and that was upsetting.

*He's as cool as a river rat and as infuriating as a peddler! Marcus has to go–leave the ranch–I'll fire him–I can do that!*

*He's playing me along like others have tried to do. I'm an oddity–a gangly female who works like a man. I'm neither attractive nor dainty and don't have a delicate bone in my body. Men aren't attracted to a woman like me.*

She threw around a few curse words for good measure then looked around to make sure Uncle John was out of earshot. She knew full well that there were no soft curls on her head. Her hands were callused. Her exposed skin was tanned from the burning sun. Her whole body was hard and toned from working like a man.

*I can only hope he'll tire of teasing me soon. I can't take these fidgety spells much longer. They happen at the most inopportune times. Maybe I'm coming down with something. I'll talk to Mary Jane about seeing a doctor.*

Today Uncle John would expect her to dress and act like a lady. He asked so little of her that she never let him down. Ruby soaked in the warm tub before the social. She did very much enjoy being soapy, clean and fresh. The heat of the water soothed away even the worst of days. Her soaps smelled of lilacs, honey, and vanilla. The scents made her feel closer to her ma. The lacy underclothes she preferred to wear were neatly folded by the tub. These were guilty, secret pleasures that made her feel womanly.

# CHAPTER 15

The annual round-up gathering had a big turnout just as it always did. The cheerful voices and laughter of friends needing to lay the hard work aside to rest filled the yard. Children ran, played tag, jumped rope, sang and stole treats. The boys chased and teased the girls and the girls squealed in delight! Whiskey ran with the other boys' dogs as they frolicked and barked after their children. Attentive mamas took turns riding herd over the happy chaos so other women could enjoy a carefree moment.

Ruby watched as Bowie and Whiskey participated with abandon. Her brother gave a friendly yank to a long rope of a braid causing the intended squeal. This was part of the reason she worked so hard to provide a future for him. She loved Bowie more like a mother than a sister. She wanted him to enjoy as much childhood and freedom as possible.

Romping with long-time friends, no chores for the day and tag would soon be left behind for the responsibilities of manhood. With age, responsibilities always took over. Today was for Bowie to have fun.

She felt the time of him needing her slipping away. Even if she wanted the lonely life of a spinster, she wanted him to find a girl to his liking and raise a family. She wanted him to carry on the family name and work this land.

Men talked of men's concerns. They told of rustlers and bandits who were hitting spreads farther to the west. It disturbed the bad memories she kept tucked away. The reports of pilfering, burning and killing caused her to replay bad images she'd tried to forget. She eavesdropped on the men as she stayed busy around them and no one seemed the wiser. She was used to hearing things men shared among themselves. Men were more interesting than ladies.

Instruments appeared out of nowhere to accompany hymns and play for the dance later. Women changed into nicer dresses and fresh aprons. Tablecloths and other bright coverings laid on the tables under growing piles of food. Flapping in the dry breeze the colorful collection cast a gypsy-like spell and a sail-like sound that snapped in the Texas wind. The winter had been long and harsh and kept community friends from getting together. This get together and the comradery brought much needed joy and warmth to every soul.

Ruby's gown was a light green calico sprinkled with tiny yellow flowers. The thin weight of the garment draped and complimented womanly curves she didn't usually flaunt. The thin fabric made her feel bare in contrast to buckskins or jeans that she usually wore. No one was surprised to see her in the dress and slippers. This had always been one of Uncle John's requirements of her when it was warranted. Everyone had seen her like this many times before and paid no mind now.

Marcus, however, was caught completely off-guard at the vision of Miss Ruby Red Blake all decked out like an angel.

*Damn, Girl! You're a beauty! Who would've thought?*

A primitive drum beat in his chest. It hammered like thunder. He actually choked on his own spit and had to cough to clear his passageway. Nothing prepared him to see her like this.

*I'd bet a month's pay you have a knife and a Derringer strapped under your skirts. You got a gun tucked in there somewhere, baby? Of course, you do. My little warden is always armed.*

When the hell did he start thinking of her as his anything? He'd admit to admiring her sand but nothing more. Try as he might, Marcus could not conceal his gut reaction to Ruby.

She caught the awestruck look on his face. He dared to look at her like a Christmas ham. He was a scoundrel! She felt the heat of mortification on her cheeks. She hadn't thought about Marcus seeing her in a dress for the first time. How she loathed men looking at her like a piece of raw meat.

Area menfolk had long since dismissed Ruby as unapproachable and incorrigible. Harley Johns didn't care. He was willing to walk through fire to get to her inheritance. She mistrusted Harley and had discouraged him at every turn. She was infuriated that a greedy man would try to take advantage of her.

# CHAPTER 16

The ranch's cowboys attended the church service if they wanted to get fed today. Cook oversaw the barbecue. Food at a community gathering was always spread out like a veritable banquet. Good chow tended to entice unbelievers or back-sliders and the aroma floating in the breeze right now wafted to them like a siren. It had the power to call in even the worst of sinners!

People were beginning to settle before the service started. Ruby's jaw nearly dropped when Marcus dared to slide in right by her on the bench. Her hackles raised at his bold move feigning familiarity and instantly, that squirmy feeling plaguing her lately was back surging through her body. Her mouth dried up like West Texas.

*Why on earth is my body disloyal to me? I truly must be sick.*

The fresh soapy smell of the man next to her mingled with the essence of leather and horses assaulted her senses. In fear of slipping over the edge of something deep, she was on the verge of panic. Her heart tapped rapidly in her chest. Ruby tried to school her mind to take charge of her body but at the moment she was too busy just trying to

breathe.

Marcus's will power was taking a beating and losing. Deliberately he'd waited for Ruby to take a seat so that he could sit down by her. She looked so all-fired soft and sweet in that green dress. The sight of her in something pretty rocked him back on his heels the minute he saw her. This total transformation had a governing effect on him. His body could feel her fidgeting on the bench and that was problematic for his manhood. She had become jumpy the minute he sat. This amused him and he worked at not laughing. He was one ornery cowboy. Obviously, he was making the invincible Ruby Red nervous. As more joined them on the bench, the two were forced closer together from each side. Both thighs, hips and arms were pressed together.

Suddenly it was Marcus who felt like bolting. The building heat within his loins made a part of him start to ache. He had never been so physically attracted to any woman. It made him weaken and sweat with randy urges. He positioned his hat in a strategic place.

He leaned with his mouth close to her ear.

"Miss Ruby, you are one fine-looking woman this morning. You're a pleasure to look upon in your girlish dress. What I mean to say is–you're gussied-up like a flower. You're the prettiest girl here and I have to say it."

He tried to eat the words that had tumbled out of his mouth on their own volition.

"Excuse me, Ruby, for saying so. I didn't mean to speak so freely. I only meant–"

"Shhhhhhhhh!"

Her head jerked toward him which was a mistake. He had not had time to move his mouth from her ear. Now their mouths lined up only a scant breath apart. She only meant to look at him sternly for the ludicrous declaration.

She stammered for a voice. No insincerity shown on his face. The earnest, anxious expression made her over-swallow. Suddenly she felt close to strangling. No man had ever dared to speak to her of such things. She had no idea how to handle his statement or his closeness.

Ruby had spent long years avoiding personal connections with random boys and men. Now one was threatening to tear down her walls and she feared being left exposed.

"I can't believe you've said these things," she hissed. "Are you making fun of me, Marcus?"

"Miss Ruby, I won't take my words back! I've overstepped my boundaries, but I stand behind all I just said, and I'll happily repeat myself. If you don't know how pretty you are then it's a real shame. You need to hear the words again and again until you believe them." His voice had risen just a bit above a whisper. Heads were beginning to turn in their direction.

"Shush, immediately! Someone may hear you," she cautioned. "We'll not speak of this again!" She glared at him long and hard for emphasis.

"First, get one thing good and straight here, Miss Ruby. You can't shush a man—leastways not one you can count on. You may have rescued me from Lord knows what and you're my boss, but I won't be shushed by you again. Twice in less than five minutes is enough!"

"Tell me. Does the man who keeps looking this way have a claim on you?"

He demanded what he had to know.

"Well? Answer me!"

"Oh! Pity sakes, you're maddening," she said tartly. "Not that it's any of your business, but that's Harley Johns. He asked Uncle John if he could marry me a year ago."

Ruby was irritated at herself for sharing such personal information. Something about Marcus Dobbs caused her mouth to open and spill over like a fountain. Where was her head for heaven's sake?

Apparently, Marcus did not find her answer clear enough and he persisted.

"And, well? What was your uncle's answer?"

"He told him that it was up to me."

"And, then what happened?"

"Oh, Lordy! I'm not married as you can see, Mr. Dobbs! If I was, you'd have heard about it by now. The truth is that I will never agree to marry anyone!"

Again, heads turned as she raised her whisper slightly. Her face was hot, and she could feel it blazing.

He heard the resolve in her declaration. "How can you be so all-fired sure you won't agree to marry someone? I know why I can't marry. With my Pa dead, I'm the one left to provide for Ma, my brother and my sister. I hate what it did to my ma to lose her husband and how it affected the whole family. I'll never risk leaving behind a helpless family like pa did.

"Now, I've told you my reason for not getting' hitched. Let's hear yours!"

As the oldest, Marcus grew up overnight with the weight of the world on his small shoulders. He took responsibility for his broken spirited ma, a bright little sister and a younger brother. There had been no one else to house, feed and clothe them but him. He'd bitten the bullet and buckled down leaving childish ways behind. In the end, he had to move away to earn enough money to support them all.

Childhood ceased for him and he didn't even remember the boy he'd once been. That boy turned to vapor as he was digging his pa's grave. Every day, he did recollect being down at the creek fishing and daydreaming without a care in the world when the smell of burning and the sight of smoke rising from the direction of home alarmed him. He ran the whole way to get there. He'd heard the screaming and crying before he'd seen the devastation.

For years he'd been drifting and was tired to the bone of moving around from pillar to post. Desperately he'd begun to hunger for more love and comfort than a good horse could give a man. He suspected he did want to take a wife and have his own family someday, but did it need to be with this contrary female? He couldn't think he needed a woman this stubborn.

Ahh–but the heart wants what the heart wants!

He took a deep, leisurely breath and smelled lilacs, honey, and vanilla mingled together to create the sugariness of Ruby. He was entranced by her. Her hands, toughened by hard ranch work, were on the small side and just right for holding. There wasn't anything about this outrageous girl that didn't define and amplify everything he'd come to admire. She'd accidentally lassoed his heart and she didn't know it or want it.

*I'm in over my head here–God, I lack the sense You gave a goat! It's not Judge Bean who holds me captive, but this peculiar girl named Ruby Red.*

Only the discovery of this bright jewel, Ruby, had gotten his attention. He was mesmerized by her beauty and fearlessness from the start. He was now realizing that he might be in love with this too-big-for-her-britches girl. He had a strong desire to take care of her. He wanted to be the one to get her past whatever had blocked her path. He wanted to nudge her forward and go along with her.

Marcus appreciated her daring uniqueness and he smiled at her guns. She could ride a stallion like an Indian, rope wild bulls before breakfast, and make him so mad that he could spit nails, but she'd caught him hook, line and sinker! Ruby was tenacious, strong and definitely sassy. It made his hand itch to spank her lush bottom to put her in her place. Her excited indignance lured his mind to places he knew he should not go but her innocence, despite her bravado, was a sensual draw.

His head had been spinning out of control since she'd ridden into Langtry on a giant of a horse that stood at least eighteen hands high. When he'd first seen her in those pants with all of her arsenal he was immediately captured. Later when she'd barked orders and ridden out of town on the big, red stallion, he didn't even mind eating her dust. He'd have followed her anywhere.

When Pete told him from the beginning that John Blake would abide no disrespect of his niece he didn't mention not falling for her. Pete probably didn't think such a thing was even possible. Working the round up had made him face the extent of his attraction to this cute hellion. He was amazed by her roping and handling of her horse and the situation. There were many men who wouldn't take on a stallion as imposing Big River.

He could hardly keep his eyes off her and on his horse and business. At first, he felt inadequate. He'd never cared what a woman thought about him before. After the initial hesitation it had turned out to be an unbelievably exciting day. They worked together like a finely oiled mechanism. His edginess quickly melted away.

The preacher had started the service before Ruby had answered his question. He'd been so lost in her that he'd heard not one word of the man's message. If he didn't get away from Ruby's intoxicating fragrance and sunshine hair, he'd become incoherent and useless. He needed to put distance between them if he hoped to reclaim his good sense. Even if this girl found favor with him, it would not go over with John Blake because he was just a hired hand. An established rancher like Harley Johns would eventually get the prize.

*Well, old Harley, not if I have anything to say about it!*

As soon as the last amen was said he turned and walked away from her without another word. The growing gap did not keep him from continuously looking for her in the mingling crowd. It rankled him to see Harley seeking her out. He gritted his teeth knowing that John Blake had already given the man his blessings.

# CHAPTER 17

She was at the drink table serving lemonade and Marcus was filling his plate with food. Going through the line at the food tables was a good diversion but he was anticipating getting a drink from her at the last stop.

John Blake studied Ruby's new fellow. He had observed his niece and this cowboy working together. He'd noticed signs of tension growing between the two on several different occasions. He'd found them sitting together and whispering before the service. He'd observed the sparks flying between them. He was pleased to no end.

He deliberately stepped in behind Marcus in the chow line.

"Dobbs–Marcus Dobbs–Ruby hired you to work with the mustangs. How are you getting along with her? She's bold and direct and some men can't take that in a woman, but she does know horses. When it comes to horses, she's the best."

"I agree, sir. It's good working with someone who knows what they're doin'. I'm a wrangler by trade and like when someone knows as much as I do. We have some of the same skills and methods based on common sense and a horse's spirit. She's left me alone with my work for the most part and Blue John is a fair stable foreman," Marcus answered.

He didn't mention how Ruby had saved him because John Blake didn't know where Ruby found him.

"I enjoyed working with her during branding. The stables are well-managed by her. You're right. Miss Ruby does know what she's doing and she's very direct about it. I respect that."

"Pete tells me you're a reliable all-around hand. This is a big spread. The vaqueros who have come in temporarily to help with the extra work will quit soon as we move the herd out to be loaded on the rails in Langtry. They'll be looking for their pay and will head out permanently that very day.

"Pete says you pull your weight and are a man of good character. He thinks you're trustworthy with a cool head on your shoulders. I need men like you around. Ruby just signed a bigger contract with the army and she's smart to have hired you. She and Blue John needed support busting all those extra horses."

More softly, John said, "I can see you and Ruby are evenly matched. I've been watching and it looks like she may have found her match. It's saying something if you can keep up with Ruby."

Surprised by Mr. Blake's praise, Marcus said, "Miss Ruby's good at what she does. I'll give her that. We do work well together, and our horses know what to do. Big River is a fine cutting horse and so is my Bob."

"He's spoiled beyond redemption, but he'll work for her." laughed John good naturedly and Marcus smiled at the obvious truth.

"Well, it seems to work for them both, sir."

As they progressed down the line, heaping their plates John Blake added, "I've noticed you patiently taking time with Bowie. In fact, he relentlessly quotes you at the supper table. Be careful what you say as it will wind up on our menu. I appreciate you taking time with him. Ruby and Bowie mean the world to me. They're mine but in truth they're my brother's children. Their ma and pa were killed years ago. Ruby has a difficult time putting the memories behind her.

"Ruby Red is a caring and generous person when you get to know her but she's complicated and hard as nails at the same time. That puts most people off, especially suitors. I encourage her to let others in but she doesn't. I saw you two sitting together this morning. Never saw such happen before. It got me to thinking that it could become a habit. The two of you being together seems easy. She's never given any other man the time of day, but she seems to pay attention to you. That's an accomplishment but confusing since the two of you look downright at odds sometimes."

"Yes, sir, there is that. She and I seem to gel and then tangle–back and forth. I irritate her and she gets on my last nerve. I'll steer clear of her. I'll respect your wishes," Marcus replied uncertain that he could keep his word.

"Bowie is a good boy. He reminds me of my little brother. He's easy to be around and eager to learn. You have a really nice family, Mr. Blake. I envy you."

"I'll remember that the next time I have to corral my niece. Yeah, for an old widower I have been blessed beyond measure. It seems my brother left me the greatest gift a man can be given. He left me his children.

"Try one of these cobblers, boy! Ruby made the cherry one yesterday."

"Ruby! Your Ruby bakes–cherry cobbler?"

John chuckled. "She's a girl of many surprising talents. You might just like her cobbler if you give it a try. She can rope and she can cook! I recommend her pie. It's really sweet and worth the effort even if you bite down real hard on a pit once in a while."

Marcus took an extra big helping of the flaky crust and

red cherries in the thick rich filling. He looked over Ruby's way.

John Blake was no fool. He knew what he was seeing. When he'd first noticed the sparking going back and forth between his niece and Dobbs, he'd questioned Pete about him. Pete was quite impressed with Marcus which was a confirmatory endorsement. Then he'd sent off four telegrams inquiring information from two former employers, a sheriff and a friend of Blake's who had some connections. Not a scratch could be found against the man's name. It was a lucky fluke that Roy Bean had jailed him even if Ruby hadn't leveled with him. Both ranch owners he'd heard from asked if Dobb's would be interested in coming back to work for them. Yes, John was satisfied that no danger would come to Ruby from this man.

One could only hope that romantic notions might develop. That is if the boy could stand up to her and he was proving to be capable of that. Any man willing to take the time to tame Ruby would have to be up to the challenges! He'd have to be tougher than her sometimes. Harley Johns certainly wasn't.

Before John turned away from the table with his heaping plate, he said, "Oh, Dobbs! Ruby may sit with whomever and talk to whomever she pleases unless I become aware of some reason she shouldn't. I won't interfere with you getting to know her."

Marcus nodded not exactly sure what he wanted do with the apparent permission. On one hand it made him think about the future and various possibilities that included Ruby. On the other hand, he leaned toward running the other way and fast. He stopped in front of Ruby for some of her sweetness but as always, he received her tartness.

"You baked one good looking pie, Ruby."

"How do you even know I made that pie? Lots of women brought pies here today."

"Your uncle pointed this one out to me. He said you were a sure enough good pie maker. A really sweet one was what he said about your pie if I remember correctly.

Ruby's cheeks blushed for the third time today and she pinched her lips together in a pout. By the perk registered in his eyes she knew immediately that he was only fueled by her indignation. She could feel the heat on her skin rising in temperature. That made his teasing even more exasperating.

"Marcus Dobbs, you're barking up the wrong tree! You always are. You best get your mind on eating! Teasing faint-hearted, silly girls may have worked before but you're talking to me now. I'm not so easily skunked by a silver-tongued devil like yourself."

"Miss Ruby, you have wounded me, but as usual it's been most entertaining talking with you." He touched his hat to his heart in a most gallant manner. "If you'd be so kind as to pour me a cup of your liquid refreshment, I will leave you to tuck into this chow. I will surely be back for seconds." He walked away with plate and drink in hand. If she could have seen his face instead of his back, she would have seen his mischievous smile. The fact he could cause her to blush gave him power over her. That was worth knowing. Without a doubt he looked forward to provoking more sass from her pretty lips.

Harley respectfully asked Ruby for three dances and she complied out of civility. During the afternoon several ranch hands boisterously spun her around the floor all in good fun.

Right now, she couldn't say who was holding her too closely, but it felt off. He'd not uttered a word of acknowledgment and had simply taken for granted she'd dance with him. In fact, he'd been rude. She had started to rebuke him but knew if she called attention to them in front of guests her uncle would be dishonored.

The man's damp hand had slithered up until one wrist was wrapped tightly in his fingers. He had astutely rendered her fighting hand useless. With his other hand clamped around the other arm, he had her sufficiently restrained.

The old dread of being held down took over Ruby's reasoning. She began to twist and pull in an effort to quietly break free from his grasp. It was only causing him to apply more pressure. She made the decision to stomp his foot and knee him hard enough to hurt regardless of the consequences. Before she could take the action, a hand from behind gripped the cowboy's shoulder. A familiar voice spoke assertively accompanied by a cold grin that appeared friendly but was not. This was a different side of Marcus than Ruby had witnessed before.

"Thanks partner! Don't mind if I cut in do ya? I promised the boss's niece a dance."

Marcus deftly whisked her away before the dumb cluck could even react to what was happening. As soon as he'd seen Ruby in distress he'd come to her side. He was surprised that it took a braced effort to break the grip on her.

Anger flashed when Marcus saw that her wrist was reddened from the man's grip.

*I'll address you man-to-man later. Ruby could have taken you but not here. I can't cause a ruckus either, but this isn't over yet!*

Marcus had been watching from the sidelines as Ruby danced politely with anyone who asked. Being a hostess, she acted accordingly but it had been pure torture for him. Stubbornly he'd been stalling to take his turn until the end of the soiree thinking making her wait on his attention might make her heart grow fonder. Now he was sorry he'd been such an ass. When the rowdy manhandled her, Ruby's face registered stress and he'd hurried to the floor. Though tempted to knock the man's teeth down his throat, this was the wrong time to cause a scene.

Ordinarily she was capable of fighting her own battles, but this man had pinned her. Panic and indecision registered on her face. That was a look Marcus had never seen her wear before. The man held her at a disadvantage and against her will. It wasn't hard to guess that Ruby was holding back not to embarrass her uncle.

The primitive urge to protect what was his swept through him as he gazed down upon her beauty. The handsome gown twirling around slender ankles all afternoon had heated his blood. What he'd planned to be one turn around the floor became the last three dances of the day. Once he held her in his arms, he couldn't make himself walk away.

"Did that trash hurt you? Are you alright? What happened exactly?" he asked.

"Nothing!" she denied.

"It didn't look like nothing to me and he was hurting you! I can still see your tender wrist. You were relieved as soon as I stepped in. I felt you trembling. Girl, don't lie to me when I ask you a question. Do you know him?"

"I don't know who he was! Marcus, you're making too much out of something that's entirely my business. I take care of myself—always have—fight my own battles. Let it go."

He let it drop for now. Dancing is a legitimate reason to hold a girl close and he was enjoying it too much to spoil his time with her. He could smell her sweet hair again, study her full lips and feel her light breath brushing his face. He wanted to give Ruby a sound kiss but wouldn't dare. He wanted to give her more than one and knew it might get him shot but oh, he did crave to cover her feisty mouth and silence it. His body buzzed with inappropriate thoughts and naturally his pants tightened.

# CHAPTER 18

At the end of the week Marcus soaked leisurely in the Rio Grande River. It was a glorious afternoon away from the ranch and he was completely alone. It felt good to clean up without tomfoolery filling the space around him. It was hard for a man to hear himself think with the constant boasting, joking and idle talk of other cowboys. He relished the isolation of this long, snaky river and the untamed land of the two countries bordering each side. The river itself was gentle and calm in some places and wild and unpredictable in others much like Ruby and that horse of hers.

Watching a fat, lazy turtle floating along, he lost himself in thoughtful consideration of that uninhibited girl.

*Now why would Ruby Red come to mind? Oh, right! She's wild, unpredictable, exciting and will cause any man who claims her nothing but trouble! She's not for me. I need a woman content to keep my house, have my babies, satisfy my needs and do what I say. That sounds like one boring woman and it sure ain't her! I'm not planning to marry anyway–so one way or the other it makes no difference to me.*

*Get your mind off her, cowboy! It's time to visit a compliant saloon girl! In fact, it's been too long without.*

He scrubbed the grime and sweat off of his muscled body with vigor and a white cake of lye soap. His dark brown hair washed clean and dripped onto his broad shoulders. As he lathered, he got an uncomfortable feeling that he was not alone.

He'd had this same feeling earlier. Riding away from the ranch he'd started looking over his shoulder. He'd not seen anything that warranted suspicion. He attributed his unease to fatigue. He'd been giving Ruby a hundred and twenty percent on the mustangs and he was worn out.

He finished up his bath whistling a soft tune. The idea that something wasn't right still niggled at him and experience had taught him to take persistent feelings of danger seriously. He systematically checked out the perimeters of the area but still didn't zero in on anything specific. It certainly could just be his imagination this time but he couldn't be sure.

Damn!

He deliberately made his way to the bank where his pistol lay within easy reach. His pants, boots and a piece of sack cloth lay beside it. Each step exposed a little more skin and dignity to the air. Being naked and dripping made him exposed to trouble but until he could reach clothes there was nothing to do for it.

Ruby had followed Marcus simply because she could. He deserved it for teasing her and it was fun. She really didn't mean any harm. The easy tracking hadn't challenged her because he wasn't trying to hide his destination. She had soon lost interest but kept going anyway out of curiosity. When she was close enough, she spotted Marcus Dobbs bathing. She should have turned back immediately out of modesty but the very idea of Marcus naked made her insides quiver in that confusing way. She was as inquisitive as any young lady about a man's body. Foolishly, she assumed that she could satisfy her inquisitiveness and he'd be none the wiser. Guilt carped at her but she'd come too far to peel herself away when it was just getting interesting. Common sense kept warning her to go home and leave Marcus Dobbs in peace.

Just thinking of catching a glimpse of his muscled backside threw caution to the wind and stupidity won out. Ruby was definitely in the wrong, but it was so worth the gamble! She had become riveted to this spot.

She knew little of physically grown men except for their strength of body. The expectation that Marcus must surely be a fine example of mature male anatomy had her risking much more than was prudent! Even fully clothed she'd noticed powerfully built shoulders, muscled chest, broad, solid back, firm middle, tight rear end and corded arm and leg muscles. How much better it would be to see the skin of the man unencumbered!

Once Marcus started rising from the river, Ruby was immediately hooked as sure as a catfish! The lure to see this virile man she admired snared her. She never thought much on what caused the attraction between men and women, but Ruby instinctively thought of Marcus like honey on a biscuit and she felt like a fly at the table. She just wanted a tiny taste of what he had to offer that made him a man and could make her a woman. Unseemly thoughts flew around in her mind when she was around him and she was weary of wondering. Right this moment, her body was fairly buzzing with what she could only imagine.

When Marcus walked completely out of the river, she held her breathe and forgot the need to breathe. The tightly curled hair on his chest created a thick, dark, mat. The hair dwindled all the way down to a thin line that led directly to a nest of dark, tangled hair between his thighs. A shock ran through her as she stared at the long, fleshy penis that did indeed make him a man.

Her rebellious body shuddered, and she carelessly lost her footing causing a slight rustle that could have easily been caused by the wind. It was time to skedaddle before she was discovered. Her heart thumped with anxiety, but she risked one last look. He shook his body to rid himself of water. A shower of water drops shown like prisms in the sun until they fell back in the water and were lost. Ruby made it to her horse with stealth and the light foot of a cat. She foolishly trusted she had not been detected.

After Marcus pulled on his pants and boots, strapped on his gun belt and picked up his rifle he made straightway to his gelding. He saddled Bob quickly, shoving his things back haphazardly into his saddle bags not taking time to pull out a shirt. In one fluid motion, he was astride and headed in the direction of the movement he'd not only heard but had also glimpsed when vegetation had been disturbed. He couldn't put off taking a serious look any longer.

Ruby, of course, was already gone and unaware that she was now the one being followed. Reaching Big River, she was off in a split second. She'd stretched upward grabbing the saddle horn with both hands and making a leap and swing that put her atop the red stallion. Big River was used to her shenanigans. He was already taking long strides by the time she landed with a slap in the saddle. She put it to him and was off like a candle in the wind. Even if the cowboy suspected someone had been watching him, he could never catch her. She'd be drinking tea in the shade looking calm, cool and in the clear by the time he rode in.

She sailed through the air with the yellow braid flying behind her. The big hat was crammed on her head and tilted over her eyes and the silver and turquoise on the band were reflecting points of light. The reflections played with the sun. This intermittent twinkling made it possible for a pursuer to get a bead on her in the distance.

Ruby made a sight on the fine animal and never once felt a need to look back. She was invincible. This cowgirl was the real deal and a force to be reckoned with! She was in control as usual! She laughed with her face almost touching Big River's neck and her shapely bottom keeping rhythm high in the air off the saddle. The horse and rider were moving as one blended force. Both of their hearts were pumping overtime with reckless speed as they moved along smooth as silk. The horse was a magnificent goliath and used to working with the girl. The giant was giving her all that he had.

# CHAPTER 19

B y the time Marcus topped the rise overlooking the ranch headquarters he'd worked up a fine bad humor. He could see Ruby had made it to the corral and was taking care of Big River. Once Marcus had been sure it was this audacious girl he was after, he'd kept his horse at a sensible speed. She could lather her horse, but he wouldn't do that to Bob unless he had a good reason. He was angry at her daring carelessness and childish behavior.

What is she–twelve-years-old?

The hot ride had wilted some of the starch out of him, but he had plenty left over to teach her a lesson. He tied his horse a ways back and slipped up to the corral behind her. Ruby had climbed up the outside of the board fence and was leaning over brushing Big River's back. She was unaware that Marcus crept up behind her and he was loaded for bear.

This was the opportunity Marcus had been waiting to present itself. He was loaded to paddle the round globes conveniently jutting out from the fence. He would set her straight once and for all. He swiftly grabbed her under both arms and pulled her down backwards before she even knew what was happening. The action caused her breath to escape in a surprised screech and dislodged her hat sending it to the ground. Once her feet landed, he whirled her around and slammed her back none too gently against the corral fence. His hard, full body lay against the length of her. She was held there with the sheer bulk of him. One of his arms was on each side pinning her with nary a chance of escape. She panicked with the dreaded feeling of entrapment. She wiggled and fought and said several unladylike things that caused his eyebrows to raise more than once as he held her securely.

She was forced to raise her chin so she could look up at him. He had to look down at her. He deliberately leaned his forehead against hers. Neither had said anything until Marcus exploded into her face.

"What the heck was that? What in the heck did you think you were doing? Have you been raised to slink around spying on people? Is that how you've been raised, or did you come up with that trick all on your own? Somebody ought to swat your bottom end good, hard and repeatedly. You need to be taught some manners and made to think about your own safety.

"You don't go sneaking up on a man when he's taking his bath. Tell me--did you see what you were looking for? Are you satisfied? You've stepped over the line, Ruby–way over the line!

"The worst thing is that you could have been hurt riding back here on that horse like a whipped-up whirlwind! Half the time, I could see daylight between your britches and the saddle. I don't know how you've kept from getting seriously injured before now. I've never met such an impetuous, impulsive, unruly, infuriating woman before. You need a man, Ruby–you're a danger to yourself!"

If he hadn't been so caught up in the heat of the moment, he might have noted the vulnerability in her eyes. "Oh wait, and let's not forget the bar room language that just tumbled out of your mouth so easily! You need a taste of soap. Oh, and I just happen to have a bar in my saddle bag but you already know that!"

"Whoa, whoa! Stop it!" John roared as he came from seemingly nowhere and caught the two mashed up together against the fence. "Would one of you like to tell me what's going on here? Marcus, you're not even fully dressed! Where's your shirt? You don't even have one on and you're crushed up against Ruby! You'd better do some fast talking, son, and I better like what I hear. At the moment, I'm thinking of killing you!"

Marcus was chagrinned to realize that indeed he wasn't wearing a shirt. The pressure of his hard body against Ruby's womanly softness registered on his brain. He knew how inappropriate this must look to her uncle. Too late he thought better of having put himself in this position. The liberties he could be accused of washed over him.

Sweat glistened on his shoulders and made the hair on his chest and the soft tufts of dark hair under his strong arms sparkle. The smell of soap from the river bath permeated the air around him. He was so close that she was barely catching her breath. He felt embarrassed and ashamed of this whole episode, but she had betrayed his trust. She had no right and there was no acceptable excuse for her part in this.

Marcus lifted contact away from her forehead and turned his head only enough to face John Blake who was definitely not a happy gentleman. Marcus held his ground and was not daunted enough to back down and release the errant girl from her comeuppance. Ruby was still held tightly and too speechless to move a muscle. He was adamant that she should be held to account for her poor behavior.

"Your niece took a ride today and followed me to the river. She watched while I took a bath. She brazenly spied on me the whole time from beginning to end. Then she blew her cover and rode back here like the devil was after her. I think Ruby needs to answer for her actions!"

Ruby still had said nothing but was fidgeting and turning to see where her hat had landed.

"She's been making a fool out of me all afternoon!"

"Ruby, I hate to think this is true, but I fear it is. If you did this, you were very foolish and rude. This is not like you. You have become unpredictable to say the least. You will take responsibility for your actions and pay the piper.

"I should have put my foot down and reined you in long ago. I've failed you and your father. It was my job to raise you right. Sooner or later I knew you were going to get hurt or into something I couldn't make go away. I'd say that's where you've landed yourself now!"

Uncle John was fuming. A couple of cowhands came around the barn to see what all the commotion was about. Seeing it was a family altercation they darted out of sight quickly but not out of hearing range. This was the boss's private business and didn't involve them. That didn't keep them from straining their ears like old women safely tucked out of sight.

"Uncle John--I--"

"Be quiet, Ruby. Get to the house. I'll deal with you, young lady, soon enough!"

At this, Marcus took a step back releasing Ruby. She ducked under an arm scrambling for her hat and high tailed it in the direction of the house. She never looked back. She was glad to escape Marcus's justified anger, her guilt and the embarrassment.

She was shocked to recognize a newfound respect for Marcus. Everything he'd said was true and he refused to back down from her or Uncle John. It was really he who'd gotten the best of her and not the other way around for a change. No man had ever been able to do that before.

Jess was standing in the yard waiting for her and he

gathered her into his arms. His sympathy caused her to release a sob. Ruby was upset and she felt safe with him. Even if she was in the wrong he would hold no condemnation against her. He always gave her unconditional love.

"Now, Dobbs, don't leave your horse waiting any longer. Take care of him and for crying out loud put on a blasted shirt! Come up to the house when you're presentable. I'll be in my office waiting for you. I am going to do some hard thinking about this impossible situation you and Ruby have put all of us in. I'm sure you know that we've been put right in the middle of a moral dilemma."

# CHAPTER 20

A grim-faced Jess let Marcus in the back door and pointed him in the direction of the ranch office without a word. The cowboy had cooled down considerably but apparently Jess was still out for blood.

If he was lucky, John Blake had called him here to be fired and to collect his pay. Heaven help him when the man finds out he's in Ruby's custody! He could never leave without facing the dire consequences laid out by Judge Roy Bean. Hurting Ruby would equal a loose rope and hanging slowly. Maybe the boss would settle for a quiet horse whipping instead.

In hindsight, he should've handled this whole afternoon differently so that it stayed between Ruby and him. Now the dice had been thrown and wiser choices were only in hindsight. The cat was out of the bag and the whole fiasco was probably public knowledge all over the Triple B. Juicy news that smelled of trouble always traveled quickly by word of mouth throughout a ranch.

John Blake was honor bound by an unspoken code of ethics and ego to deal harshly, man-to-man, on behalf of his niece's honor. Everyone would be waiting and watching to see how this would be settled. No way was there a good ending in sight for Marcus.

"Well, I see you're at least dressed now," John huffed as he ran his hand through his hair already ruffled from the repetitive action. It was clear that he'd been doing some heavy thinking.

"Sit down.

"That was quite a problematical spectacle between you and Ruby today. It suggests monkey shines to me and everyone else. I've talked to Ruby and she denies none of the allegations. She backed up everything you said happened and I know you did indeed speak the truth. You went about addressing it the wrong way.

"I'm sure every hand is recanting the story and the retelling has been fragmented a dozen different ways. This doesn't bode well for Ruby's reputation.

"We usually don't have this much excitement around here. It's a good thing for you I discovered the two of you going at it instead of Jess. He's Ruby's champion regardless of whether she's in the wrong or not. Ever since the kids came to live here, he's doted on them both like a grandfather. It's entirely possible he would've shot you first before asking questions. Keep that in mind as he may still feel he has a score to settle with you."

Marcus sighed, "Yes, sir–I figured as much.

"I apologize sincerely to you and your family for my conduct. I meant no disrespect to Ruby's person. She infuriated me and my temper took over before my head took hold. Please, take my word that nothing untoward happened today on my part."

"Nice try but not good enough! Nice words won't fix this. From my perspective I have to make a decision that protects her from scandal. Short of shooting every man on the ranch, I don't have many options."

The boss looked at nothing for a few minutes before he

shrewdly spoke. The silence had been louder than thunder in Marcus's ears. This man was obviously out for blood too. Marcus would have to take whatever Mr. Blake decided.

"It's important to me that you understand who Ruby is. She looks like a woman, acts like a strong woman and is a formable opponent but emotionally she's still a little girl. She's stuck somewhere in the past and hasn't been able to escape what holds her there.

"She was nine and Bowie was two when they came to the ranch from along the West Texas New Mexico border. Bowie was still sucking his thumb. My brother was getting his family and a horse ranch started there. A bloody tragedy took place and unfortunately Ruby witnessed it. It left her feeling like the weight of the world rested on her shoulders alone.

"I got to the children as quickly as was possible but not before she became the mother of a baby. She never felt carefree enough to be the little girl she was supposed to be after that. The weight of the world rested on her shoulders or so she truly believed. She would not allow me or anyone else to bear any of the responsibility for her."

Marcus identified with feeling that kind of weight and accountability. "She was awfully young to give up the ways of a child. It's not how things are supposed to be. Can you tell me what happened to their parents?"

"That's a very horrible story. Bandits rode in and looted everything. Ruby apparently witnessed every detail of the cold-blooded murders of her parents and the burning of her home. Based on the condition of the bodies, these evil, ruthless men made them suffer for a long time.

"Somehow she managed to hide Bowie and herself, but she watched as bandits held her ma and pa at gun point while they ransacked the place.

"No doubt my brother was made to witness them torture his wife. She was probably raped repeatedly and eventually her throat was slit. They set the buildings on fire and stole the stock.

"Ruby's never spoken of it to this day except for bits and pieces to Jess. I mostly got her story from him. I pieced it together with what neighbors reported and the authorities thought. What she witnessed contaminated her perception of men, her role in life and her attitude in general.

"After witnessing the carnage of it all she took Bowie and the colt she'd saved up to higher ground and sheltered them in a cave. They were all she had left to hold onto, and she did it with her life.

"Neighbors from miles away saw the smoke and investigated. It was obvious that vicious bandits had hit the ranch."

Marcus broke in. "I've heard accounts of raids like the one you just described. It's unbelievable a little girl was able to salvage so much and make such a difference. It's incredible."

John continued, "The neighbors had to ride quite a distance to reach the aftermath. Finding only the two adults' bodies caused them to assume the children had been taken. No need to organize a search party for them was seen so there was none. That was an unfortunate mistake.

"A few weeks later a goat herder heard a baby crying and investigated. Thankfully he found them before it was too late. Ruby must have had a hell of a time keeping them alive. The kids were suffering from exposure and all three of them were thin and dehydrated. I've often wondered how much longer she could have held out.

"They were placed in the care of the nearest town's preacher, and I hit the trail the same day word reached me that they were alive. Let me tell you, I prayed all the way there."

Marcus's face looked sympathetic. "That must have been quite a message to receive."

John heaved a sigh as he reflected. "I was a thirty-three-year-old widower and had only seen Ruby once when she was Bowie's age. She couldn't possibly have remembered me. I had no earthly idea what I was going to do with two little orphaned children, but I knew they were mine and I wanted them.

"Jess and Mary Jane were already working for me at the time. Jess was the bunkhouse cook and his wife was keeping the ranch house up for me. I sent word back for Pete to hire a replacement bunkhouse cook immediately and to move Jess to the house kitchen. I asked Mary Jane to make ready one room for the children. It was plain Ruby was not about to be separated from Bowie. I told Mary to buy whatever was needed to make two children feel at home."

"They were lucky to have you take them in," Marcus said.

"They were and are my flesh and blood. There was never a question about bringing them here to raise. It took over a year for Ruby to trust any of us even a little bit. She wouldn't leave Bowie unattended with anyone. She carried the boy on her little hip, and they spent as much time as possible following me around. I think she saw her pa in my face. When the baby slept, she spent time with the colt. I'm sure you've guessed the colt is Big River!"

"I've wondered about their bond. They have a communication that's uncanny," Marcus said.

"That's right.

"It was so sad to see a little girl who couldn't relax and play. Ruby was never a lighthearted little girl after what she'd witnessed. At least her nightmares eventually subsided."

Marcus took the boss's story and mulled it over. "In view of all this tragedy she has grown into a courageous and remarkable woman. Ruby is a survivor to be admired."

John Blake nodded. "Ruby soaked up everything she could learn about this ranch. Bowie naturally began to learn too since he was always with her. She gave him attention in spades with love and patience. Ruby has all the forbearance in the world for her little brother.

"It was amazing the way she could take care of him and sit a horse at the same time. I was surprised that she could even ride but she's a natural born horse woman. I put her on the smallest, gentlest little mare I could find. That little mare is still here on the ranch and greatly honored. She'd wrap a scrap of cloth around her waist and Bowie's to keep him from falling."

"My brother must have taught her to ride and allowed her to follow him around. She already knew some of the very basics of ranching. I can almost hear him explaining the how and why of doing each chore. Ranching is in Ruby's blood. She lives it and sleeps it.

"She was so independent, and I didn't see the harm in letting her do as she pleased. This land soothed her, and I wanted her to find happiness. She and Bowie inherited their knacks with horses from their pa. It would have been robbery if I hadn't allowed them to use their talents."

"I can see you've done what's best for both your niece and nephew. Ruby being so headstrong is not your fault and, in many ways, it serves her well."

"I felt so much compassion toward them and before I knew it, they'd stolen my heart. I changed the name of the ranch to the Triple B marking it as much theirs as mine. This is their home forever. They belong on this land."

Marcus spoke as if thinking out loud. "Ruby walks alone because she trusts only herself. Learning to believe in outsiders is not her strong point."

"You're right, Marcus. Ruby Red isn't willing to take chances when it comes to other people. She has never let many in proximity of her. She always expects the worst."

# CHAPTER 21

"Ruby's been restive since the day you came here. It's not altogether a surprise that this has finally come to a head. You've got her confused. Her predictable order of thinking has gone haywire because she's enamored with you. She's never felt an attraction to a man, and it's thrown her off course. She doesn't know how to deal with you.

"You got the drop on her this afternoon which means you outsmarted her. Oh, she deserved your anger alright, but her submission has cost her dearly. She's never given into anyone else before.

"I've been worrying over Ruby's future for a while now. She's spoiled with freedom. She's repelled all the young men in the territory with her mule-headedness. She's bested them in one way or another. A man needs to feel swaggering and her temperament does not allow that. They need ordinary women to stroke their egos and she is the extraordinary!"

Scratching his chin, John Blake added, "I've been thinking she needs a strong, self-confident man to husband her. One who'll love her the way she is but one who will take her to task. A man she can respect and can't run over.

"I saw that in you today, son. You're a man who can keep up with her and not be hesitant about putting a foot down firmly. She also needs a husband who appreciates her backbone–an extraordinary man."

Beginning to smell a rat, Marcus tried to redirect John. "That's a tall order for a man. Ruby is—well–she's tough–Ruby is–well–she can be difficult! What about Harley Johns? I noticed him admiring her. She said you told him it was up to her if she wanted to marry him. He seems decent enough. Maybe you should talk to him again." Marcus tried to ignore the way his chest was tightening when he thought of Ruby marrying someone besides him.

"Good try, Marcus," John laughed loudly. "Harley doesn't have the first notion how to handle Ruby. He's mostly interested because his land butts up against this ranch. She'd have him running in circles the day after the wedding. She has to have a real man—one tougher than she is. You're right though. It is one tall order to find such a man.

"I don't ever want to see her spirit broken, but I do see that it's time to rein her in. She needs to face her softer side. There's a whole lot of love in that girl. When she gives it over to some fortunate man it will be like a rainbow of colors bursting across the prairie after a rainstorm. Her time is now at hand to settle down and give over at least one of the reins to a husband. I wish she could see that on her own, but I've given her enough time to choose for herself. I know now that with God's guidance I'm going to have to do the choosing."

John explained, "Uncertainty motivates Ruby more than any emotion. For all her boldness she is afraid of relinquishing control to a man. She saw men violate her mother, kill her pa and take everything away that belonged to her and Bowie. She associates men with pain and suffering. A very special man is needed–one who can show her love–a good husband who will take care of her. Do you understand where I'm going with this, Marcus?"

"I think so, sir, but this afternoon, I strong-handed her, and I imagine she is scared to death of me now. She won't ever forgive me. She probably loathes me for it."

"The verdict is out on that," Blake answered. "I don't see it like you do. I think it was the best thing that could have happened to Ruby. You certainly held her attention and she needs limits established.

"I've had my eye on you, Dobbs. There's a strength and a determination about you that I like. The first time I noticed the two of you together I had a feeling Ruby had finally found who she wanted.

"To be on the safe side, I sent telegrams to the last two spreads where Pete said you've worked and made inquiries about you. Your employers couldn't say enough good things about you or your work. They each wanted to know if there was a chance you'd come work for them again! You are respected as a good, dependable man of integrity.

"Marcus, I know about the fire and your pa's death. It's ironic that both you and Ruby suffered loses about ten years ago. I know that you've taken responsibility for supporting your family ever since. For a young boy to face the world at fourteen and start earning a living for a family tells me that you're made of iron. It's about time for you to catch a break, I think.

"Ruby has never shown an interest for any other man except you. Unless I've got it wrong, you deserve that interest. Even before witnessing you together this afternoon solidified what I've been thinking, I figured you're up to the task of taking her to wife if anyone is." His voice trailed into silence and he looked at nothing for a moment.

Marcus took the break as an opportunity to get a word in edgewise. "Mr. Blake, there's one thing you don't know about me. Ruby found me in–"

John held up a hand to stop him. "No, Marcus! It won't work. Roy already told me all about you being in his cage at Langtry. He said you hadn't done anything that he could see. That's the only reason you got your horse and gear back. He wouldn't have let Ruby ride off with a real outlaw. If you were a threat, you wouldn't be standing here now. Roy can be accused of a lot of things but being careless with my niece's safety is not one of them. Ruby doesn't suspect that I know where she found you." John winked.

John took his time pulling out two cheroots from the humidor on his desk. The look on his face was lighter and younger suddenly. He lit his smoke with a sulfur match and held the small flame out for Marcus to light his.

Taking a long draw and exhaling, he continued with outright straightforwardness. "Marcus, I have decided to give you permission to court Ruby with the intention of marrying her."

"What?" choked Marcus who was waylaid by John Blake's words.

"I don't have a hankering to court your niece or any other woman for that matter. I'm just a hired hand with nothing to offer. I'm not looking for permanent ties. I don't even stay put in one place for long. Besides, handling Ruby would be like trying to put a cat in a bag! I admire her spit and so many other things about her but I'm a bachelor through and through. I will live single like you. Besides, most of my earnings go to keep my own family's heads above water. I don't have much left to provide for me much less a wife.

"She'd never have me anyway. You saw today that she hates me! She's stubborn as a mule and refuses to take direction from any man, especially me. She clearly doesn't want to marry either. It's just that plain and simple. She's too wild and spoiled. I'm too impatient and hot-headed to deal with her shenanigans. If I ever do court a woman, I'd have to have one a might more compliant and domestic than Ruby."

"Dobbs, you should have considered the consequences before you accosted Ruby in my own yard! Let me be crystal clear on where I stand and explain it so that you comprehend the severity of this situation!"

The older man enunciated every word slowly and deliberately. "You've narrowed your possibilities considerably. You allowed Ruby to see you naked, you man handled her, and you weren't wearing your clothes. Your face was touching hers and maybe there was kissing and squeezing. I can't be certain where your hands and mouth had been roaming before I discovered the two of you together.

"Surely, you know," John raised his voice for effect, "any father would conclude that his daughter's honor has been compromised. You've sullied her reputation, Marcus Dobbs. You took advantage of Ruby and ruined her chances to marry. You put on a display of disrespect in front of many witnesses.

"Should Judge Bean get hold of this news he'll cook your goose! As her guardian and his old friend, I'll make sure he knows if you don't willingly fall in line. He'll marry you and Ruby before sundown without a single question."

Marcus just stared at Mr. Blake in disbelief of what he'd just heard.

"Are you suggesting a shotgun wedding, sir? You're stretching this whole thing way out of proportion. Please, reconsider."

Desperately, Marcus pointed out, "Who's to say Ruby would even consent to my attentions? She's never struck me as a girl who's looking to be courted. Did I mention that she doesn't even like me? I wouldn't have any idea how to change her mind. Ruby doesn't respond to sweet talk. Boss, are you sure you want to go down this particular road?"

"Marcus, how would you know Ruby doesn't like sweet talk? Have you already tried it, perhaps?" John asked arching one eyebrow.

"It's within my rights to order you to do this. Matters like this are usually decided between men over a cigar and a drink. Women don't have too much say once they've been compromised and their reputations are at stake."

He pulled down the bourbon and two shot glasses from a shelf and poured the glasses full.

"Drink up, boy! You've got courting to do. Oh! By the way, I do see signs that she's taken a shine to you. She just doesn't realize it yet.

"Jess already knows to set an extra plate for supper tonight. It's time for the whole family to get better acquainted."

# CHAPTER 22

S upper was as awkward as Marcus had imagined it would be. The food was mouthwatering, but it didn't reduce the tension. He tried to concentrate on the bounty of thick beefsteaks, mashed potatoes, beans and rich butter. Everyone but Ruby and Jess made small talk in an effort to make him feel welcome at the family table. It looked to him like John Blake was the only one having a fine time and it was all at his expense.

Ruby sat cold-shouldered, stiff and straight. She only picked at her meal. Her agitation fairly hummed in the air. Somehow, he doubted that Blake had clued his niece as to the consequences of her poor judgement. No doubt, she would be exploding and throwing things at this very minute if he had.

Marcus couldn't help noticing that she'd had a bath since the afternoon's misadventure. He could smell her fresh, appealing sweetness and see the scrubbed pinkness of her skin from across the table. She was wearing a blue pin-striped skirt and a white shirtwaist. It wouldn't surprise him if Blake made her come to the supper table dressed like a lady every evening. He noticed that her firearms were missing but he didn't, for a minute, imagine that she was not armed. He suspected that feminine attire might be the decorum her uncle insisted upon for the supper table, but Ruby wouldn't go unarmed for anyone. This state of dressing like a lady was a darn good rule in his opinion. Ruby was lovely like this.

Bowie plied Marcus with questions and the chatter broke some of the strain at the table. He held back no hero worship as he chattered throughout the entire meal. He was delighted to have his new favorite person on stage. It was obvious Ruby found her brother's adoration to be a burr under her saddle.

The boss over road Bowie's enthusiasm long enough to ask Marcus a few questions for the family's benefit. They heard he'd always wanted to raise horses and he'd been wondering what kind of colts and fillies Big River might sire if he was bred to some select mustangs based on colors, muscle builds and temperaments. Marcus mentioned a couple of the strong, wild mares he'd been working. He even shared that he was going to try and convince Ruby to hold onto them for breeding stock.

This was the only time Ruby's face reflected interest. A glimmer of softened, attentiveness lit her eyes and her appetite seemed to pick up. He felt compassion because she'd been humiliated by the hornet's nest she'd stirred up this afternoon. All that had transpired was of her own doing and the desire to offer her comfort caught him off guard.

He'd really misjudged his feelings for the girl. Why did he wish things were different and that she was interested in him? She wouldn't even look at him. *Oh, Lord, just wait until she discovers what's been set in motion by her actions today. She'll shoot me for sure!*

The two of them had indeed created a heck of a mess! This was one big royal muddle to be fixed. Blake had them strategically sitting across from each other. It was effectively like rubbing salt in raw wounds.

Mary Jane and Jess were obviously cherished members of the family even though they weren't kin by blood. They'd been on the ranch since before Ruby and Bowie had come here. The couple acted like grandparents to the siblings.

Marcus recognized Mary Jane as a kind, nurturing woman. She did subtle things to soothe the tension at the table. She asked Bowie how his day had gone since he'd been out with the boys checking fences. She didn't ask Ruby about her day. Marcus knew everyone but Bowie knew exactly what Ruby had been up to.

This couldn't have been the first time this audacious girl had landed herself in trouble. He smiled but couldn't think of why the thought of past mischiefs should amuse him. The poor man who finally did take her to husband would have a never-ending headache. Her impulsive behavior and stubbornness would try the forbearance of a saint.

Jess's wrinkled and pruned face looked like he'd swallowed a persimmon. Marcus wondered if the old man would ever forgive him. No wonder John's hair was graying with this patched together family to ride herd upon. He surely had his hands full, but for some reason he always appeared to be a contented man. How could he not be bogged down with the burden of it all? What was Marcus missing?

The climax of supper was the dried apple pie with heavy cream. Even Ruby practically licked her saucer like a kitten. Jess and Ruby began clearing the table simultaneously, marking the end of the meal. Marcus took this to mean that the strained getting-acquainted exercise was over.

A great meal beat getting fired, but good chow didn't make the prospect of getting married to a she-cat any easier to swallow. This afternoon's altercation had created a dilemma of gigantic proportions for Marcus.

"Marcus and I are going to take a walk," John announced tersely as he scraped his chair back. "Jess, you outdid yourself as usual. No one ever goes hungry around here!"

Mary Jane excused herself to their private cabin while Jess busied himself washing up the dishes and getting things lined out for breakfast. Marcus exchanged quick glances with Ruby which caused her cheeks to blush a deep red. The signs of her embarrassment were very tiny kernels of payback for the trouble she'd caused.

She looked away so quickly that Marcus actually smiled. Maybe he wouldn't be able to completely get even with her, but he could delight in taking little nibbles out of her hide. He could deliberately cause her agitation for his own amusement. She'd started this game and he could be ornery too if that's how she wanted to play.

Without another look at him, she told Bowie to get his spelling out so she could help with his word list. Bowie rolled his eyes but got right up and did as he was told.

Wise boy!

# CHAPTER 23

John pulled out two more cheroots as Marcus followed him to the main corral fence. He offered the smoke and a light to him. They stopped at the far side of the corral facing the house. They each propped a foot on the lowest board and leaned over with the top rail supporting their arms. It was a typical masculine pose of men mulling something over. They smoked for a while without speaking a word. Marcus's thoughts were smoldering like wood in a banked stove.

*Am I dreaming this quagmire? I've fallen right into John Blake's trap. He's bamboozling me into marrying his niece. The man's desperate to find a husband–she's a tough one to marry off. I fell right into his well-played hand!*

Marcus tried to sort the situation and could find no way out unless Ruby refused the arrangement. The worst to happen would be that he'd end up with a smart, pretty, courageous, talented and cantankerous woman who would defy him at every turn.

It was a definite plus that she just happened to be a part of this big spread. It also didn't hurt that she loved raising horses as much as he did, and she was established and good at it to boot.

Ruby never warming up to him as a suitor would be the best possible scenario. Things would all blow over and John would forget the whole sham. He could go back to living his simple, free life and being alone again. When Marcus looked at the current state of affairs both ways it muddled his resolve. To be truthful with himself he didn't know which way he wanted it to turn out for sure.

He couldn't deny that his recently intended was quite pleasing to look at and he did admire her overabundance of grit. Her early, tragic story was compelling, and it made him feel even more protective of her than ever. Maybe it was time to settle down. He was tired of being alone. Ah, hell! What was he considering?

Breaking the silence, Marcus once again tried to offer a heartfelt apology as a peace offering.

"Listen, John, I need to apologize sincerely for taking Ruby to task today. I had no idea of the tragedy she's survived. I'm sure I must have startled her senseless. I'm truly sorry about that and I will apologize to her as well. I guess my pride was hurt more than anything. My temper can outrank my good sense. I can see how the show looked damning like you said, but I swear I did not make improper advances toward your niece. I would never do that to any woman."

John just chuckled and passed a pocket flask to him which he accepted.

"You're the first man besides me who's ever stood up to Ruby's guff. I must concede that you're far better at it than I am. For a minute there I thought you might actually paddle her, and she did too. I'll be the first one to admit that's exactly what she needs. At least you got her attention today and made a definite impression.

"I told her to make amends with you. She'll have to think about it for a while, but she'll apologize in time. It may sound strange but I'm glad you got her to focus and held her accountable for her reckless actions. She's had limited experience with strong-minded, virtuous men if you get what I'm saying.

"She remembers her convoluted version of what she saw as little girl. She's used that to paint all men with the same brush and that's unfortunate for her. It's got her all twisted up inside.

"She was just curious about you being a man today but that doesn't excuse her indecency. It is worth noting though that she chose you to gander at and not some other cowboy. You are her first, you know? She's had cowboys around her for years and never took an interest in any of them that I know."

John laughed again.

"She's one wild and exciting woman for the right man. I'll be the first to admit she's a challenge, but I think you're up to it. I can't say for sure if she was born daring or if it has more to do with what happened to her folks. The terror of what happened was too much for an innocent child to witness. Her world was literally torn apart and it might cause any of us to have a chip on the shoulder."

Marcus understood this trauma because of the disappointment he'd carried for so long over his pa's death. It would have been so much worse to come to terms with it if he'd had to watch multiple sufferings as they were taking place. Thank goodness his little sister and brother had run far enough away to be spared the seeing. His mother had seen it all. Even the thought of it made him shudder.

He found himself engulfed in that overpowering feeling of wanting to protect Ruby from any more hurt.

John spoke again, "Ruby and Bowie have been brought up on this range running free. There's not much Ruby doesn't know about ranching and Bowie's learned from her. The truth is that I respect them both for their tenacity and especially Ruby's sand.

"Don't be thinking she's not soft-hearted and nurturing

like a woman should be. You'd be selling her short. She tries hard to hide that gentler part of herself but down deep it's there. Just look at the love she's put into raising Bowie.

"I've always appreciated and loved her just the way she is. Her undaunting spirit is most admirable. She has unprecedented courage to face what must be faced and to survive anything at all costs. It's worth the time it will take for you to really get to know her."

Marcus had witnessed the kindness she had shown the downfallen woman in jail and how the sweetness of it had tugged his heart strings. He remembered how she had rescued Bob and him from their predicament.

He just had to ask purely out of curiosity.

"How old is she?"

"Ruby is a lot of different ages, but in actual years, she's nineteen. Emotionally she has the horse sense to be thirty but the foolishness and innocence at times to be no more than thirteen.

"I figure you to be about twenty-six, Marcus."

"That I am. If I had a choice in this courting scheme you seem determined to hold me to, I'd decline. The truth is that you've got me over a barrel and you and I both know it. Since I have no choice other than getting married tonight in Langtry or at least horse-whipped by the judge, I'll give courting a shot. I make no promises as to how Ruby will take to it."

About that time, the focus of their discussion broke out from the backdoor of the house letting it slam hard behind her. She hurried to the stable and disappeared inside. Both men watched in silence. Marcus reached again for the flask and gulped a big, fiery swig of liquor that made him gasp for a breath. John could not suppress a victorious chuckle at the man's surrender.

They both were visibly startled when Ruby Red rode out of the barn on Big River at top speed with her skirt and hair flying in the dimming light of dusk. From a distance they could hear her yell out like a heathen as she leaned low.

"Mercy me!" Marcus exclaimed out loud. "I 'spect it's time for me to take a ride and explain some things to her.

*That crafty old son-of-a-bitch! He's holding all the high cards and I've got nothin'. I wish I'd never met Ruby! Why couldn't I have just left well-enough alone this afternoon— just this once? She didn't hurt me and I'm not a modest man.*

Continuing to mutter crossly, Marcus turned Bob and rode in the direction Ruby had disappeared. They needed to have a serious talk as soon as possible.

# CHAPTER 24

A breakneck run after supper was necessary to ease Ruby's frustration. Uncle John made her mad enough to chew leather sometimes. He'd invited Marcus Dobbs to join the family table as a way of putting her in her place. She got it!

He wanted to remind her that he's the boss. She didn't need a recap of the hierarchy around here. She knew he was the authority on the Triple B. She never usurped his position unless the times she'd done as she pleased counted.

She sounded childish even to herself!

Raising horses was what she most wanted to do on the ranch. Being left alone to do it was just easier for everyone concerned.

Big River sensed Ruby's mood the moment she entered the barn. His muscles tensed and quivered as she jerked the saddle in quick, impatient motions. She pushed him in a mad dash out the door in less than record time. He was allowed no warmup. The big horse's adrenalin pumped into his veins giving the necessary punch required.

Ruby demanded instantaneous action from the stallion tonight, and as always, he gave his mistress everything she wanted. She was often hell bent on putting distance between herself and whatever phantom she was escaping. It was a common game horse and rider played together. The speed of the chase burned restlessness in her that was going to explode if not expended. The pressure in her head was painful and her neck and shoulders were tense.

Uncle John and that cowboy were leaning smugly against the corral fence. She couldn't miss them as she charged out the kitchen door. Uncle John looked pleased when he was holding an Ace! Marcus had the countenance of a man stuck with a bad hand and no money to back him up.

When John Blake wanted to finagle things his way, he could stack a deck slicker than grease. That wasn't to say that he was a cheat, but he did have an uncanny way of making the stakes work to his advantage. She wondered what the two were negotiating as they stood there like two roosters squaring off. Intermittent red flashes declared they were smoking, and she figured drinking too.

They looked like a couple of Indians smoking a peace pipe! *They both think they can tell me what to do. How has it worked out for you so far, Uncle John?*

Ruby never slowed Big River until they topped the rise to the east. She didn't push him anymore as they headed to the tree line in the distance and he knew exactly where to stop. She rode just under the tallest tree, her tree, and stood on the saddle after dropping the reins signaling him to stand in place like a statue. Faithfully he stood steady as a post while she reached up pulling and swinging herself onto a sturdy limb. Her skirt made the maneuver a bit more difficult than usual, but she made it work.

This was another game they'd played often over the years. Big River knew the drill perfectly. He'd graze and come back to the same spot when she whistled and do it all in reverse. Higher and higher she climbed out of sight like an agile lumber jack.

Most of the trees were scrubby in this part of Texas but this one was an ancient, mighty oak. As a kid she'd carved her initials into the trunk claiming ownership and it had been hers ever since. This giant was familiar with her and she trusted its faithfulness. They were bonded hand to bark and bark to hand. Ruby had watered it with her tears and stripped it with her angry words many times. It was the place to hide, lick her wounds or mull over her most private thoughts. At present, she was perched as high as the highest branch that would support her weight. From this vantage point she felt safe from trouble on the ground.

Ruby knew she was difficult, and few were willing to look past her irregularities to see the real Ruby who lived inside herself. Her anomalies were justified by scars from facts, memories and heartaches from the past. These things rolled around and blended to create the illusion of her outside-Ruby. She couldn't understand most of it. Lately, old memories were getting vaguer around the edges but no less hurtful.

*Are my memories a reality or only the imaginings of a nine-year-old? Did awful things happen the way I remember? They haunt me and I want to scream them away!*

Thank God that Jess and Mary Jane had the patience to help me through the roughest spots of growing up. Dear Jess sat at the base of the big oak many times over the years listening to me. His counseling was always gentle.

Ruby had always found it hard to articulate what she needed to get off her chest, but Jess always gave her whatever time she needed to get it out. She'd thrown fits of anger, grief, confusion and defeat. He listened until the current storm passed then they'd talk until she was calm enough to descend and give the world one more chance.

Jess was her mighty oak in the flesh. How she loved that

old weathered man with his strong, tall trunk and safe branches! He knew more about her than even her loving uncle who was so very dear to her heart as well. Jess could usually talk her down. He comforted her through so many things that threatened to crush her soul and he cooled the sting of her fears.

As dusk was settling from the terrible day, she sought the peace to put to rest the humiliation of her trespasses against Marcus. She wished she'd never followed him to the river. She wished she'd never even met Marcus Dobbs! Why did she take such liberties on his privacy? What a terrible lapse in judgement! She wanted to erase the vivid images of what she'd seen. New feelings and questions were jumbled together in her head like fallen leaves.

What was happening to her? Uninvited, assorted and mismatched yearnings flew through her like shooting stars! She could not banish the naughty thoughts. She was feeling that fidgety unsteadiness that came and went at will. She understood not one implicit thing that passed between married men and women, but she had an educated idea based on the horses.

She wasn't totally innocent. Ruby was a horse breeder after all, but the idea of anything beyond working beside a man left her drawing a blank. She felt in danger of losing her footing. Living a normal life scared the starch out of her.

She saw the author of her distress in the far distance of dusk. He was headed her way on Bob. He sat his horse well. Ruby knew him as a persistent, hard-headed man who could get the best of her anytime he wanted. She could only imagine what he would say to her tonight if he could find her. He'd not had his whole say yet. He was here to give it to her now. Marcus seemed to always get in the last word, but she wouldn't give him the satisfaction this time. She couldn't allow him to see her injured and doubting herself. She'd sit tight until he turned back. He'd never think of looking up. She'd have the advantage over him for a second time today.

*Talk to the wind, Cowboy!*

On approaching the tree line, the first thing he noticed was Big River grazing a ways to the west. The girl had to be close. He scanned the area for signs, but it looked like she had vanished into thin air.

After a few minutes of looking he felt skunked and called out, "All right, Ruby, you got me again. I know you can see me. Come on out. I want to talk to you–that's all– just talk. I won't touch you. I swear. I'd enjoy wringing your pretty little neck, but I promise not to do it. There's something important we have to discuss."

Nothing! Not the snap of a twig, a flutter of motion or the sound of a disquieted animal broke the stillness. Only Big River lifted his head briefly to look his way. Marcus waited, became impatient and then got irritated.

"Okay, girl, have it your way again. Don't go getting too used to calling all the shots. You're in for a rude awakening if you do. I'll catch up with you later." He rode away as she watched his back.

Damn, she was a peculiar female! John Blake was loco to think she can be courted and tamed. Hog tying her comes to mind. What man would sign up for this exacerbation? Ruby was impossible, but he had to make John believe he was trying or he'd never get out of this mess.

# CHAPTER 25

Ruby put her horse away and walked through the kitchen door after admiring the stars that had popped out. She stopped short when she caught Marcus's silhouette sitting at the table with a cup of coffee. He was waiting for her no doubt.

"What are you doing in my house?" she snapped. "How could you possibly have the brass to just walk in here without an invitation?"

"Well, it is true. I did let myself in and poured a cup of coffee but I'm practically family, you know. No one but you has an objection to me being here." He grinned the most charming, lazy smile.

"In all fairness, I did try to speak with you in the meadow earlier. I couldn't locate you, so I decided to wait here. I knew you'd show up sooner or later."

Despite the strain between them, Ruby couldn't help but notice how fine he looked. With that unsettling wave of credit came the recollections of her inexcusable rashness of the afternoon. She felt her face growing hot and hoped he couldn't see in the dim light.

Would she ever get his naked body out of her head?

"What are you trying to say–practically family? What's that supposed to mean? I've never been good at riddles so speak your mind plain out," she snapped.

"Well, apparently, I am privy to pertinent information about your near future that you don't have yet. I'm not surprised that Uncle John hasn't mentioned anything about the changes he's made in our relationship. I wondered if he would fill you in or if he left that for me to do. Looks like it's my job.

"I won't mince words. It's important to make sure you understand. I want this whole arrangement clear to you right up front. It's not my way to speak indirectly and tiptoe around difficult situations. I'm going to put all the cards out on the table so there are no doubts about the farce that is about to be played out."

"What in the living hell are you rambling on about? Just say what you're itching to say and quit beating around the damn bush with veiled remarks."

"It seems, Miss Smarty Pants, that you have put me–us– in a precarious situation with your disregard for etiquette. Your uncle feels determined that you were compromised by mc today. He mentioned escorting us into Langtry immediately for the judge to marry us." Marcus drawled his words out southern style.

"What—the—horse shit? You're a liar! No!"

"Now, now, Ruby, that's enough of the bad words and rude accusations for one day and I don't ever care to be called a liar ever again. Is that any way for a proper young lady to speak? I'm beginning to understand more clearly what your uncle meant about your manners needing to be smoothed and tamed. It would serve a girl as pretty as you are to clean up her verbal responses. You may have to have your sweet mouth washed out yet and I can certainly do that for you, anytime."

"How dare you threaten me so crudely! I'll speak anyway I please. Who do you think you are? I wouldn't marry you if you were the last man on earth! You'd be my last choice. I'd sooner take Harley over you!"

"As a matter of fact, I suggested old Harley Johns to do the honors instead of me. It turns out that your uncle doesn't think he'd have the slightest idea how to handle the likes of you. For his own sake, cut the poor man loose once and for all. You'd wear him out in less than a year. Have some pity, woman! He's no match for the spoiled baby you are, darlin'!"

"Oh, and I suppose you think you are?" she hollered.

"As another matter of fact, yes, but I haven't decided if you're worth my time or not yet," he baited her. "It would take a lot of concentrated effort to get you in line and break your many bad habits."

"I'm not worth the effort–what bad habits? Why, you lowdown polecat! I would never permit you to try to, nor could you–get me in line! You are one arrogant, overbearing piece of horse–"

Holding up his palm toward her in warning, Marcus said, "Stop right there, Ruby! I'm sorry you feel so strongly about me. According to the boss I may be the last chance you have. It seems you've bested all the other would-be suitors in the territory.

"Being that's the way it is, your uncle seems to think that it's up to him to decide how to best protect you from further damage to your reputation and to secure your future. Man-to-man, he and I have discussed the legal complications arising from your little stunt this afternoon. We, the men, have made the decisions and arrangements necessary to restore and protect your honor."

For a moment, Ruby was so taken aback by what he'd said that she just stared at Marcus.

"Dammit! This sounds like something he'd do!" she exploded.

"Now, there you go again, little Miss Ruby, with the careless talk. I really do believe you do need a real man to take you in hand. Remember, I told you once that I won't be shushed. Now I'm telling you that I don't back down from an obligation either. I'm not a Harley Johns or one of the young bucks around here who's not up to the task of straightening you out. You'd best watch your step around me, pretty lady, and pay close attention to what I'm telling you."

If looks could kill, Marcus would have been a dead man that instant. He even thought that there was a possibility she would climb over the table and go for his throat. He knew she could make a weapon appear faster than most ladies could pull out a hanky. He hated the prospect of having to restrain her again. He didn't want to keep over-powering her, but Ruby's conduct was a trial of his patience.

"Hold on a minute—now–," he said putting both palms out and up to calm her rage. "I was able to talk your uncle out of a shotgun wedding for the time being but only by agreeing to court you properly." Marcus smiled that charming, warm smile that was endearing and most infuriating at the same time.

"I told him that I'd sooner court a badger--two badgers, as a matter of fact, but he didn't act like he heard me. So, I feel it is only fair to inform you of my intentions to comply fully with his demand for all appearances. I feel it's a viable compromise. For me, it's either that or be married to the orneriest female I ever met or be shot for trying to get away. I'll say one thing for you, Ruby Red, when you set a ball in motion; it evidently has to roll until it hits the wall.

"I figure if we act like I'm courting you and you can keep yourself from falling for my charms this will all blow over soon enough. That would satisfy your uncle that he'd made an effort to see you settled. Don't you think, Ruby? Then I'll be free to go back to my life and you can go back to your unladylike mischiefs."

Ruby just looked at him. Her anger was going past a

simmer to a full, rolling boil.

"Enjoy your coffee, Mr. Dobbs. Close the door on your way out and don't let it hit you in the ass!"

She stalked out of the room leaving him to reflect on her sharp, sassy mouth.

Marcus smiled genuinely this time since no one could see him. If he could keep her off-center enough so she'd stay fuming, John could see that this match was not workable. He wasn't even sure if he really wanted it to fail, though. She was one little spit fire and that amused him while it also riled him in a most peculiar way. It might be interesting to play along for a while and see what happens. A little sparking couldn't hurt either one of them and she appeared to be a girl who could use a thorough kissing. He certainly didn't mind being the one gentling her a little, after the strong-arming she'd taken from him this afternoon. He was truly regretful about that now.

If he couldn't shake this nuptial-sentence, the Triple B would become his home and that had a certain appeal. The sunshine-haired girl with the gutsy personality was indeed thought-provoking. He actually laughed out loud, recognizing that this whole power struggle might even be fun, gratifying and full of pleasant surprises.

From there his thoughts took a nosedive and twirled around and down like a dust devil. He found himself thinking at the beginning again and chasing his tail back to where he had started. He sure was uncertain for a man who'd just said he never backs down.

# CHAPTER 26

R uby was way over on the far side of furious at Uncle John, at Marcus and at herself as well. She'd baited a trap and the two men had discussed and decided her fate as easily as dividing up a side of beef!

She saw a dim light coming from his office and found her uncle sitting at his desk and told him as much. He sat quietly and let her rant. He'd heard enough crossing of the words coming from the kitchen last night to know how she felt about the corner she'd backed herself into. He raised his eyes to her once in a while and nodded to confirm that he was listening. She continued raging into the air throwing her hands and pacing back and forth. Steam was rising! He had to struggle to keep a straight and serious face during some of her most ridiculous spouting. Ruby had always reacted this way when he issued an ultimatum.

As she finally began to wind down, he softly said, "Sit down, Ruby, honey." He waved a hand to the chair. "Are you quite finished? I think you've run out of ammunition. Listen to me for a minute.

"Look at me," he emphasized sternly, "and listen."

Uncle John's tone confirmed that nothing had been

changed by her tirade. It also confirmed that he wasn't going to take any more disobedience from her. Not being able to think of one more thing to add she did give him her complete attention. At first, she glared at him but as her angst cooled her face softened. She could never stay angry with this dear, kind man who looked so much like her pa. He'd given his whole heart and home with open arms to Bowie and her. He'd devoted his life to them.

She remembered the day he'd come to claim them. She had been awestruck by his resemblance to her pa from the very beginning. She'd sensed right off that this man meant safety to Bowie and her. He'd never pushed for her to conform or change the way she grieved. This kind man gave her the time needed to digest the bitter disappointment and adjust to all that had happened. With him she felt protected and it was the reassurance she'd needed most.

His strong arms had engulfed Bowie and her immediately. He had bent down and taken her in one arm and Bowie in the other squeezing them close and kissing their heads repeatedly as if they'd always been his. She was so exhausted from keeping everything together that she only recalled laying her head on his shoulder and giving into a deep, fatigued sleep.

When she finally woke up, Bowie had been tucked in beside her. The bed was clean & soft. The hat with the turquoise band was in easy reach. Uncle John sat in a rocking chair right beside the bed. He was reading from the Bible. It was something so much like her pa would do.

He had taken them to the hotel to be cleaned up and allowed to rest. A sweet, grandmotherly woman was hired to care for them. New clothes and a few books and toys were purchased for them. Delicious soups, breads and other soft foods were plentiful. He coaxed them to eat often during the next several days. He said that they needed to make up for the meals they'd missed. Their glasses were kept full of cool milk. A kind old doctor came and checked them over periodically. One day he declared them fit for travel.

Uncle John encircled them in a secure cocoon of love, security and acceptance. They'd been with him ever since. Together they formed a family on this ranch. Not once had he complained about taking them in as his own! She always listened to this good man, taken his words to heart and tried not to struggle too hard against his wisdom.

"Ruby Red, you and Bowie have been here with me for a long time now. In fact, I've had you as long as your folks did. I was a lonely, young, widowed cowboy when I brought you to live with me. I had no idea how to take care of children, but I knew the minute I laid my eyes on you that you were mine. You and Bowie needed me, and truth be told, I needed you. It wasn't long until I realized that we made a home together, and you became my children."

"I know that, Uncle John," she choked.

"I've let you have your way in most everything, Sweetheart. I've put up with your mule-headedness and encouraged you even when I should have put my foot down. I've allowed you to run loose on this ranch and take care of Bowie as if you were his ma. You've shouldered responsibilities that a young girl shouldn't have been allowed. I've let you take on managing the horses in whatever way you've seen fit even when others counted it as foolishness," John said. "I've come to respect you for judgement in their regards.

"Ruby Red," he added tiredly, "you've grown into a beautiful woman right before my eyes, but the story can't stop here. I won't let it! It's time that you marry and start your own family. I won't live forever.

"It will take the right man to be good enough for you. You're strong, smart, a skilled rancher and I'm sorry to say that you are spoiled rotten."

Ruby begged, "Please, I don't need a man--to--"

Uncle John broke in before she could finish. "Yes, Ruby, you do. Sometimes, we don't always understand what's best for us. I've chosen not to remarry all these years, but God in His infinite wisdom is causing even me to rethink things. He's made me realize that He gifted you children into my care but it's time to secure your futures and mine. It's not right for us to end up alone without the love, companionship and the protection of a good mate.

"It's my job, my duty, to see you well-matched and married. Marcus Dobbs will do right by you and he'll love you and Bowie. He likes the things you like, and he even will allow you to keep ranching right beside him.

"The time has come for you to build a strong, full life with a husband and to have children. You can do that right here on this land that you love so much. You can continue to do the things you love and be happier than you've ever imagined if you'll just let go of the past. This ranch belongs to you and Bowie when I'm gone and to your children when you're gone."

Sadly, he said, "If nothing else, I owe it to your ma and pa to see that you and Bowie have chances for full, normal lives. Your folks loved each other with their whole hearts. I remember the affection and respect they shared. Do you? They would want you both to have that kind of love too."

Ruby nodded. She'd heard the anxiety in his voice, and she wanted to make it right for him.

"What you did yesterday was wrong in so many ways. Your behavior was inexcusable and not without serious consequences. Marcus was right when he said that you needed a thrashing and I should have let him do it. However, you're too old for a hard spanking to fix things. Your reckless actions have put me in a difficult position as your guardian. You're not innocent anymore and surely someone has to answer for that. It's my job to see that this situation is resolved properly. You keep in mind, young lady, that you are the one who caused this mix-up! If the fire isn't put out appropriately your standing in the community will be ruined. You don't realize it now, but a lady's reputation is of the utmost importance."

Ruby studied the tips of her boots truly feeling contrite.

"Just give Marcus a chance. Get to know him and discover the things that I see in him. It could be, Ruby, he understands you better than anyone else could. He's grieved his own hurts. Find out what they are. He has dreams that parallel with yours and he's more than willing to include Bowie in them.

"I've done background checks on him and know that he comes from good stock. I know that he's shouldering honorable responsibilities that he has never shirked. Before you mention it, I do know about his unfortunate run-in with the judge and I don't hold that against him.

"He is, in fact, an excellent man and well thought of wherever he's gone before. He's a hard worker, bears up under his tasks, understands ranching, loves horses and he's looking for something to sink his teeth into. You two have a lot of common ground on which to lay a foundation."

Uncle John added, "Continue to trust me, Ruby. I would never ask you to consider a less than worthy suitor who could make you happy. You're too precious to me for that. I've been waiting for someone capable to catch your eye and Marcus Dobbs is the one. I've seen the sparks flying between you two. I've seen you talking and sitting together. I certainly know that you are drawn to him as your actions proved yesterday! We won't even go into that scandal-in-the-making!

"The point is that you chose him. You've singled him out from the herd. You give him more attention than you've ever given to any of the others put together. Have faith in the Lord's plan. Have I ever asked anything of you that I did not ask God for guidance, first?"

"No, no, Uncle John, you never have," she whispered as she rose and fell into his arms laying her head on his shoulder just like all those years ago. A single tear rolled down her cheek and wet his shirt. She suddenly felt exhausted.

"Oh, Uncle John, I love you. I love you so much. If you think this is right, then I'll at least try. That's all I can promise to do."

A tear leaked from the gentleman's eye. "Just give him a chance to court you and don't kill him. That's all I'm asking of you. Take the risk and let him reveal himself to you. If nothing comes of it, I won't say another word about it. Do this for me and your parents' memories if not for yourself and Bowie," he said. "Even Jess is beginning to approve of Marcus and that's saying a lot," he chuckled.

"Okay, I will do as you ask. I'll try to keep an open mind. Be warned though that he rubs me the wrong way. I'm not even sure why but he rankles me so. It's going to be hard to get past that. I can't make promises as to how well this will turn out."

John smiled as she got in the last word. He hugged her to him smelling the sweetness of her hair. He shook his head. The cowboy had his work cut out for him and she wasn't going to make it easy. She had a thick, stubborn line drawn around her heart that would be difficult for Marcus to penetrate.

"That's my girl, Ruby! This cowboy is a gentleman and if he's not then I'm sure you'll set him straight! Just don't be too hard on him." He sighed.

# CHAPTER 27

The next day did not dawn peacefully but erupted in violence unexpectedly. The bunkhouse grapevine had been full of activity. The boys were ribbing Marcus first thing, laughing riotously and all the friends he'd made were in his private business! No one was going to let this news go by easily.

A couple of them had overheard and seen parts of the confrontation. Everyone had garnered some semblance of truth and several elements of pure fiction. The most popular consensus was that Ruby had seen Marcus buck naked and John got his shotgun out. The tale was embellished until it had become full of discrepancies, but all versions ended with Miss Ruby being betrothed to Marcus. It was all in boisterous and outrageous fun.

Not one man had given even a glance to the shadow hovering in the dimly lit background of the bunkhouse. Why would they? He was always ignored. The sullen, stormy, dangerous look on Jake James's face would have sounded an alarm if any one of them had noticed him. Hate and murderous, treacherous fury shown on his tight face. A soon-to-be-explosion of gigantic proportions was simmering and building.

Marcus could take good-natured bunkhouse ribbing and he was trying to be a good sport as the boys continued to turn up the heat on the fiasco at the river. None meant Ruby any disrespect nor spoke anything directed at her personally. They all liked her. No disrespect was meant, and no offense was taken as they continued to pester him. The razzing was all done in a jovial spirit of brotherly friendship.

All at once, the bunkhouse went deathly quiet as a surreal scream careened from the depths of the room! Out of nowhere Jake sprang forward with a din of revulsion blowing forth from his mouth so thickly that a haze of smoke was reported later by many of the witnesses. Whether this vaporous cloud was real or imagined remained a question.

He'd finally revealed himself. His dark, secretive presence was now exposed in the light for all to see. Obscenities upon obscenities degrading Ruby's character and person fouled the air. The filth labeling her as a loose woman spewed out of the devil's own mouth. The cowboys all clinched their fists as a unified force but stepped back instead, giving Marcus the room needed to fight alone for his woman's honor. It was his unspoken right. The group took a deep breath almost as one and held it. A vacuum-like atmosphere was created in the room for the moment.

In shock and anger, Marcus propelled from his seat at the table so forcefully that his chair was knocked backwards onto the floor with a deafening scrape and crash. He glared at the monster ready to fight. The two roosters squared off with each other and started stepping. There was no doubt that a cock fight was in the making!

"Who are you? Wait, you're the jerk who strong-armed

her at the dance. Damn you to hell! Take your filthy words back now! Apologize!" Marcus bellowed. The man gave no answer to the question or responses to the demands. Neither did he make any indication of backing down. His face was reddened with adrenaline and his countenance was firm as iron.

Pete called out, "I'm sorry, Marcus–I should have gotten rid of him already–he's crazy."

"Yeah–that's right–he's an asshole–give him a beat down, Marcus–make 'em pay," the boys spoke out.

James fanned the already hot flames by declaring, "I own that tart. She's mine! She lifts her skirts willingly for me every time. She always likes it rough with lots of pain. That woman has sexual appetites the likes of you would never be able to feed."

Marcus's had heard enough. His hands flew out and grabbed Jake's collar on both sides gagging him. He hauled him out into the yard with the man's boots dragging and scraping across the floor.

Pete made no move to intercede and signaled the boys to hold back assistance.

The battle was on! Marcus, in his fury, easily overwhelmed the low-life, weak-kneed trash with the first knock-backs. Being a big man, he usually held his strength in check but this foul-mouthed, lying devil had crossed the invisible line of no return. All rules of fair-minded play fled in the rapid flood of Marcus's boiling blood. He wasn't even thinking rationally, and the fiery flow of adrenalin seemed to have tripled his strength and speed. He was out for blood and restitution.

His rapid-fire fist came up under the man's chin three times in the same place. The sickening sound of cracking bone sounded like firecracker snaps. The repeated impacts thrust Jake backwards violently. The idiot fell in a pile like dung at Marcus's feet.

Not yet gratified, Marcus jerked him up from the ground

by the hair of his head. His whole body went airborne as he dove full force into Jake's middle cracking ribs and knocking him down again. Marcus followed him with a bent knee landing all his weight like a sledgehammer into the man's gut. Jake lost his wind in a whoosh and before he could breathe again, Marcus hurled a blow to his head in a swift punch resonating the distinct crack of an eye socket.

During this melee, Jake had landed a couple of sound blows into Marcus's eye with surprising force. It was enough to cause a long, deep split in the flesh above the eyelid. It sent warm, stinging blood spilling over the already swelling eye.

John and Jess showed up called by the noise of the other cowboys rooting for the cause. Both fighters looked spent. It was obvious that Jake James could take no more pounding.

John nodded to his foreman that the fight was over, and Pete stepped forward to pull Marcus off the other man. Several of the boys stepped in to help separate them. The cook started looking over the extensive damage to the barely conscious villain. The loudmouth plainly had a broken jaw, split lip, battered face and broken ribs. His midsection had taken a powerful blow as well. The brutally beaten Jake James was holding his rib section and stomach area. He was writhing, groaning and vomiting onto the ground. He was spitting up blood.

Pete helped Marcus limp over to the boss and reported briefly.

"Jake was shooting his mouth off about Miss Ruby. He was insisting several foul and rotten things about her. If Marcus hadn't stopped him, I would have, or the hands would have. Jake had unquestionably asked for trouble but why, I don't know. It was Marcus's place to shut him up and I didn't interfere."

While Jess was looking at the split above Marcus's eye and his busted lip, his skinned and bruised knuckles were bleeding, swelling and stiffening painfully. John put a hand on the cowboy's shoulder and could feel the tension rippling through his muscles as the adrenalin was still pumping.

"It's alright, son. Take it easy now. Settle down. I would expect nothing less from you under the circumstances. Not one thing less! You did right by Ruby.

"Thank you for standing up for her. I would have done the same if I'd been here. No man is gonna' get away with slandering my niece like that. Everyone here just saw for sure how you feel about Ruby. After the story of this fight is chin-wagged around, nobody within a hundred-mile radius will question her honor or that you'll defend her."

John told Pete, "Have Cook do what he can for the man and then settle up his pay. Collect his belongings and load him in the back of a wagon. Take him off of the property as soon as possible.

"Meet with the boys and inform them the dispute has been settled. Tell them I'm aware of the details and indebted to Marcus and stand behind his actions. Tell them not to discuss this any further. I want it kept quiet for Ruby's sake.

"Put Marcus up in the main bunkhouse after Jess doctors him. He'll stay there until he's back on his feet.

"Pete, you handled all of this just right. You and I talked about firing this man. We just waited a little too long. It's my fault." John walked away leaving Jess to work on Marcus's injuries.

"Come on, Boy." Jess took Marcus up to the house. He pushed him to sit at the kitchen table. After evaluating the damage, he had Marcus hold a cold compress to the eye while he got the whiskey and his medical bag. The kitchen was empty except for them.

Marcus's eye had swollen shut and was a deep, oozy purple. Jess poured Marcus a double shot of whiskey. "Drink this down fast."

He cleaned his face and hands. When he poured whiskey on the wounds Marcus let out a few choice expletives, but Jess didn't respond. Instead, he poured the glass full again. "Drink this down," he ordered. Then he filled it for the third time and pushed it on him again. The result was that Marcus was suddenly feeling fuzzy and the pain seemed farther away. Jess's voice was receding as well.

Before stitching Jess applied more whiskey to the cut which caused Marcus to gasp and flinch slightly but the liquor he'd guzzled had taken the sharp edge off the pain or maybe it took his caring away.

Jess unsettled Marcus and turned his chair around so he could lay his throbbing head back on the table and have it supported. Well-practiced stitches swiftly closed the wound and the bleeding slowed to seeping. He again pushed whiskey down his throat.

He spoke sternly and loudly enough to get through to the inebriated cowboy. "I'm going to walk you over to the bunkhouse and put you to bed. I'll be over later to check on you after I get breakfast cleared away and something started for supper. Cook will keep a real good eye on you in the meantime. Don't leave the bunkhouse without Cook or me with you. Are we straight on that?" Jess barked.

Marcus woozily nodded his heavy head in agreement and winced with the dulled pain the movement caused. He was nauseous from the injuries, the doctoring and the whiskey. He didn't argue about being put to bed, but he wondered if he'd make it that far.

Jess led him to an empty bunk and told Cook to give him another dose of whiskey should he stir. He loosened his belt, pulled off his boots and covered him with a blanket. Marcus never moved a muscle until noon when he was dosed again with more whiskey. It rendered him unconscious a second time.

Jess came over in the afternoon to check his handy work

and was relieved to see no sign of festering. His eye was a wet mess but that would take some time to dry up and heal. He reapplied the salve and clean bandages.

Marcus's head was pounding, and he was aching all over.

Jess cleared his throat and said, "Marcus that was a fine thing you did standing up for Ruby like that. That little girl has had a harder time than most and doesn't deserve no kind of loose talk or ill-respect to plaque her. Just so you know, she ain't never even thought of being with a man. I just wanted you to know and also, I'm grateful to you. I've had a hand in raising her and I'd kill for her myself. Stay here until tomorrow for sure. Go back to work in the stable whenever you feel able after that. There's no hurry, mind you! Boss won't care you taking time off to heal if you've a mind. I'll check you again early in the morning before breakfast. In the meantime, get word to me if somethin' don't feel right."

Marcus's head hurt like a son-of-a-gun and he figured it was a combination of the whiskey as well as the damage and doctoring.

"I couldn't let that lowdown bastard or anyone else make slanders against her. I know she's an innocent. I knew he wasn't telling the truth. He deserved to be shot for the indecencies spewing out of his filthy mouth. It makes me furious all over again to think about it. It's good he's gone from here."

"John told me you and Ruby might have some tender feelings for one another. I know the two of you haven't decided how it's gonna shake out yet. Give her some time to come around. She can be thick-headed and awful difficult but that's how she's coped with what life's throwed at her. She didn't deserve no trouble she's ever had."

"Say, that's the first time you ever called me by my name."

"Maybe–I don't rightly recollect," the elderly man huffed as he was leaving.

"One more thing, Marcus, don't hurt her or you'll be fighten' me next time. Be careful of her heart."

Marcus thought he should be a big enough man to go back to work right away but the dizzy head told him otherwise. He took another swig of rot gut from Cook and rolled over in bed facing the wall. He didn't wake again until the boys straggled in from work. He was feeling a might better except for the hangover. He was able to move around some and get to the table to carefully eat some grub. He turned in again soon after that. Every man commented on the sad state of his eye and thumped encouragement and approval on his back. No one mentioned the reason for the fight. They'd put it to rest just like Pete said the Boss wanted it.

Ruby was well aware that there had been a bunkhouse brawl the morning before which resulted in fisticuffs. Fights happened on occasion but this one was different. She couldn't get any details about it from the usually chatty cowboys who were always eager to talk. Nobody was talking which was most unusual. Marcus never showed up for work and Blue John said that John had him doing something else for the day. That seemed a little odd, but she didn't question it. Something must have come up and he was needed

Marcus walked into the stable about one o'clock the next afternoon and Ruby saw his face. There was a bandage above the eye that was swollen shut, his lip had been busted and it was swollen like a melon. His hands were tied in a colorful array of clean rags and he was walking stiffly. She knew straightaway who had been fighting yesterday and she had a pretty good idea over what. Uncle John had apparently shielded her from the ugly truth. No wonder Marcus never showed up to work yesterday if the fight included him.

She was sorry to see that Marcus was injured and asked, "What were you fighting about, cowboy? I hope that the other guy got it worse."

"Nothin'! How do you know I was fighten'? It could have been a door I stumbled into."

"Nope–don't think so, cowboy. I imagine I do know what it might have been about without you tellin' me. Let me have a look at your eye."

"No, leave it alone! Quit fussin'! Jess is tending it just fine," he grumbled.

Ruby, never being one to leave anything alone firmly grabbed his shoulder with one hand and his chin gently with the other. Liking the feel of her touch he allowed her to have her way. She could smell the fresh whiskey that Jess had used to clean his stitches. She was close enough to get a strong whiff of it on his breath too. She looked his injuries over carefully and Marcus took the chance to study her face with his good eye. He felt the calming gentleness of her touch. He couldn't help but enjoy having her so near for a moment. After all, he'd fought to the death for her yesterday. Well, very nearly!

She took a step back looking deeper into the building behind him for a moment. Then her gaze focused on him again. "I'm so sorry, Marcus. I surely am remorseful at the muddle I've triggered for all of us. I wouldn't blame you for despising me now. I try not to cause awkwardness on the ranch among the hands or the family and it looks like I've put you right in the middle of trouble two days running.

"Uncle John said that I owed you an apology about my willful and selfish behavior. After having time to think more about it I don't believe just telling you that I'm sorry is nearly enough. What I did at the river was impulsive, embarrassing for you and wicked for me. It upset you and rightly so. It shamed my family and me. It's forced a situation that's not fair to you. It seems the whole ranch knows about my foolishness. You were right, you know. I am an impetuous, impulsive, unruly and an infuriating woman." She looked down contritely. "I am truly sorry."

He took a step closer to her and she didn't back up like he'd expected. He lightly lifted her chin with a wrapped knuckle. "Did I say all that, Ruby Red? Mostly, you're just unruly and too big for your britches," he whispered so close to her ear that she could feel his breath on her cheek. He reached out and touched her sun-blonde hair and wound a piece around the tip of his index finger giving it a teasing tug.

"While we're making confessions, I owe you an apology too. I was way too high-handed and brash with you after I chased you back to the ranch. I was angry that you tricked me, and I over-reacted out of pride. I should never have put my hands on you and been forceful. I hope I didn't hurt you. Can you please forgive me? I have regretted it ever since it happened. You must be wary of me now and that's unfortunate for me. I don't ever want you to fear me again. I promise I would never hurt you intentionally. Don't fear me. I could never hurt you or stay mad at you either, Sunshine Girl."

He reached up and just barely trailed a finger down her cheek, "I'm sorry about the kitchen-talk too. I knew you'd hidden from me in the meadow and it galled me. You do tend to confuse me and my good sense flies right out the window.

"Your uncle will calm down and maybe rethink his mind on making you let me court you. How about if we wipe the slate clean right now and just try to work together and get along? I want you for a friend but never an enemy."

"Starting over sounds good," she agreed. "We'll be around each other every day working with these mustangs. We ought to have better manners than they do. It would make things go a whole lot easier on us and the stock!"

She took one last look at his sore eye and moaned shaking her head. Marcus thought he saw moisture in her eyes, but she turned and wiped it away quickly.

After the confrontation, the day progressed peacefully. Time was spent on each horse in training. They were turned out in the pasture to graze and rest as one-by-one workouts were finished. The stall mucking and laying of fresh straw were the stickiest jobs of all, but all hands pitched in to help. Water containers and grain bins were refilled before leading the horses back into their respective stalls. The stock was anxious in expectation of the routine food and drink that awaited them.

The stable crew was hot, dirty and tired since they'd only broken for a half-hour at dinner. Ruby had begged Marcus to take off early, but he wouldn't hear of it. He had kept his eye bandage covered with his bandana to further help to keep the dirt and sweat from entering through it.

He and Ruby hadn't exchanged many words that weren't associated with horses since the morning's truce, but things were easier between them. Little needed to be said as they each carried out their own tasks.

Ruby talked over what needed to be done tomorrow with Blue John and then started for the house as soon as the last horse was stabled. She stopped in her tracks and turned around sharply to face Marcus again. She looked at his bandages thinking that the injuries must still be very tender. She was filled with the shame at her part in the trouble all over again.

"Marcus, come to the house for supper if you feel like it. I'll ask Jess to set a place for you. It's another small way of saying just how sorry I am. Your eye must be a mess and I'm responsible. I've seen men fight over women before and I've never understood why girls think it's flattering. I like you and I don't want you to get hurt on my account. You should have just let it go. I can take care of myself."

"I could never let it go, Ruby. I could never do that and leave you to bear the brunt of such boorishness. I couldn't let your innocence be trampled by careless words. I never want you to be upset by anything as long as I'm around."

Ruby's cheeks blushed at his sentiment. She was further surprised that his thoughtfulness filled an empty place within her.

He smiled to see the color deepening in her cheeks and was surprised at how much he liked being the one to put it there. Suddenly, he was truly looking forward to eating at the family table again. "Let me get cleaned up and I'll be in. I smell an awful lot like a horse right now. We both do!"

"Yeah, well! I wouldn't know since you're the only one I can smell!" she tossed back and they laughed

It felt good to both of them to let go of animosity and always striving to be self-justifying. It felt happy to laugh and feel the beginnings of a warm friendship. The air had been cleared of the troubled tensions.

"Oh, and Ruby!" She stopped without turning around. "Just so you know, I don't despise anything about you. At least you're not predictable like every other woman I've ever met," he grinned, shaking his head. "You're never boring my rough little Ruby. You're never boring!"

# CHAPTER 28

Bowie was all about Marcus's swollen eye and his bandages at supper. He could hardly contain his hero worship. He was full of information about Jake's departure and freely sharing the true and the untrue.

"I saw him leave the ranch yesterday and he looked way worse than you, Marcus. I wish I could've seen that fight! They say that you were a fightin' Son-of-a-Gun!"

"That's enough, Bowie," Uncle John cautioned sternly. "We won't be hearing any more about it at the table or anywhere else for that matter. It's all done. You'll eat your supper now if you know what's good for you."

As a peace offering to soothe her brother's rumpled feathers, Ruby immediately gave the boy a worthy assignment to divert his attention from his dressing-down.

"Bowie, that little sorrel mare with the golden mane is ready for you to finish. You know it's for the wife of the Postmaster in Langtry. It's ready for you to lady-break and train to a side saddle. You need to teach her to pull a buggy too. You're the best there is at that.

"You'll be going into Langtry when it's time for delivery. You'll settle up the bill and you can keep the money this time. I know you have a list of things you've been wantin.' A new rifle is one of them."

Bowie beamed at the important assignment. It was a fact that when it came to finishing a horse ready for a lady or a kid, Bowie was the best. Nobody could break a horse to pull a buggy any slicker than he could either. His sister had indeed straightened Bowie's bent feathers and sent his thinking off in an entirely different direction.

In no time he'd have the gentle mare used to flouncy skirts, sudden noises and all sorts of things. He'd teach her to neck rein with the slightest touch. He'd ride her with a fluffy parasol snapping open and shut. He'd tie shopping packages and crinkly sacks on her side saddle and back and get the mare ready to calmly face anything town could throw at her.

Ladies and kids asked a lot of silly things from their horses. He'd even tie paper flowers and bells on her bridle. No man wanted to put his family on a jumpy horse. It was important.

"Uncle John," Ruby said, "tomorrow after breakfast we'll turn four new horses out with the working string for the cowboys to rotate. They're ready to be ridden around seasoned mounts while they're working and used by different riders."

Looking at her plate she added, "Marcus, please let Pete know they're out there to be used."

John and Marcus exchanged glances and Marcus gave a business-like nod to Ruby.

She said with conviction, "Marcus, you have been incredible help with the horses. You know what you're doing. You're better than any others who've worked for me excluding Blue John, of course. I have to be loyal to him. He thinks like a horse and works magic with them.

"Uncle John, we're making faster progress than ever before. Even with Marcus not feeling his best," she smiled.

"Tomorrow, Marcus, pick out four more green mustangs

replacing the four we're rotating out."

Continuing to talk to her uncle she said, "Four more in the stable are just about ready for the general string too. We've been able to increase the production of salable mounts. I'll be ready to more than meet the larger contract with the fort and deliver on time."

For the first time, Marcus felt the pleasant warmth of Ruby's acceptance. She was giving him praise and more responsibilities. Her expert skills and experience gave the recognition teeth. It had been a pleasure working with Ruby and Blue John. They both were exceptional wranglers. He hadn't realized that she was paying much mind to what he was getting done but apparently, he'd been wrong. She was giving him credit for knowing the business and for being able to work independently.

It was evident from the beginning that Ruby was the queen bee of the stable. He had fully expected her to dog his every move with overbearing orders and demands but that never happened. She respected and valued his judgement and that made Marcus work harder for her. She was graciously willing to give an ear to his ideas and consider them. He smiled with gratification to be trusted with her much-loved horses.

Warm cinnamon cake was served for dessert. When all had finished eating John asked Marcus if he cared to go outside for a smoke. Marcus spoke up without hesitation and said that he and Ruby had planned to take a walk. He looked at her when he said this and though there was no such agreement Ruby nodded in collusion. No one suspected there had been no joint plans made beforehand.

Not interfering with their walk, Uncle John offered, "Well, how about you, Bowie? You're not ready to smoke yet but we could go out and look at the horses. We'll take a gander at that mare you'll start on tomorrow. Maybe Jess has an apple you can give her. All females respond to gifts!" Bowie grinned from ear to ear at the special invitation and humor.

Based on what he'd seen and overheard at supper, John surmised that Ruby and Marcus had come to an understanding. He could not have been more pleased. He had a good feeling about how things would turn out.

Marcus held the door open for Ruby. She looked tempting in the blue gingham she was wearing with her thick yellow hair tied back in a shiny, matching ribbon. When she put on the softer, feminine clothing there was always a fairy-tale-like metamorphosis. The girlish attire transformed her as dramatically as a caterpillar changing into a beautiful, fragile butterfly. He wanted to touch but knew it was best not to risk spooking her. She was still more than a little leery. It would take time to earn her trust in all things. He had mishandled her before, and he aimed to make amends.

She wasn't so different from a young filly always shying at the same spot in the road. The only way to get a troubled horse over a recurrent fear was to keep taking it closer and closer to the trigger point until it could finally see there was nothing so bad after all. Then he could calmly be ridden past it. He realized that he would gladly tutor Ruby gradually and gently until she could get past her anxiety of submission.

As they walked toward the water tank Ruby talked freely of the mustangs. She wanted to know more about the breeding matches he had in mind for Big River.

"I've been thinking about the roan and the black. Those two mustangs are resilient, particularly strong-muscled and full of heart. We should really consider them to mix with Big River's bloodline."

"Together let's look at them tomorrow," she bubbled with an eagerness that completely threw his heart off-guard. Marcus automatically returned her smile with equal enthusiasm and reached for her. He took one of Ruby's hands lightly in his, but she pulled away and broke the connection in a heartbeat. The link he'd so briefly made with her was lost. He was instantly regretful he had rushed her. Ruby Blake was going to take patience.

"Ruby," Marcus called out lightly as she turned and headed for the house. She stopped in her tracks but did not turn around. He waited but realizing that her back was all he was likely to get he spoke. "You'll see what I mean about those mustangs. It will be nice to look them over with you tomorrow. The right timing will be soon. They'll be ready for fall breeding."

Assuming he was finished she continued forward at a more relaxed pace. Not letting her get away with running from him that easily he called out causing her to pause in stride again. "Wait up, Ruby."

She waited while he took his own sweet time catching up to her. He calmly stepped around her and turned until they were standing face to face.

"I'm not fond of talking to your back. To my thinking you could at least try to meet me halfway. Don't make it a habit to dismiss me by turning and walking away. It's not something I'll likely get used to, Ruby."

Ruby's lower lip swelled out just a bit in hint of a defiant pout. He saw her tenderly through his heart's eyes. Just before opening her mouth for what he was sure would be a saucy retort, Marcus whispered close to her ear. "Now, Sunshine Girl, if you keep sticking that cute little lip out at me, I'm liable to do something you might not want. A cowboy can only take so much teasing from a pretty gal."

Rendered speechless she sucked her lip in immediately with a gasp and walked around his imposing figure. She wanted to get away from his overwhelming attention.

*Don't kiss me! I can't–surely you won't–I won't permit it–pretty–did he just call me pretty again?*

She'd never thought of herself in terms of beauty. Uncle John had told her she was pretty, but she assumed him obligated to compliment her! She'd never been kissed and hadn't figured an opportunity would ever come up.

She could face danger head on. That had always been easy. This was not! She looked upon Marcus's battered face. He bore the painful mark of defending her honor. Not soon enough she realized that she'd tarried too long to show her indignation. Silently she turned back to the house and started walking again.

"Oh, and Ruby," he said softly. She stalled in mid-step and turned her body ever so slightly trying to avoid encouraging Marcus. "Good night! I'll see you in the morning. Thank you for the dinner and your company."

She shrugged her shoulders, nodded her head and stepped forward. This time she made it all the way to the door and smiled a tiny bit without him knowing.

Marcus stayed behind rolling a smoke and winced at pain that was an unpleasant reminder of the fight. He let his gaze follow the girl as she entered the house until his vision was blocked by the closing door. Like a love-struck boy he stood and wondered which set of windows belonged to her. On a juvenile impulse he walked to the back of the house and stood at a distance letting the shadows of dusk swallow him whole. He didn't have to wait too long until a lamp was lit in the last windows on the left. Ruby's curvaceous silhouette was his reward. For some reason he lingered until his roll-your-own was spent and the fire had been ground out with the heel of his boot.

He was surprised to see the dark silhouette of a man approaching him from the direction of the back door. He recognized John Blake. Marcus was chagrinned to be caught across the yard from Ruby's windows.

"What are you doing out here?" asked John as his eyes followed Marcus's line of vision to Ruby's window where the soft light still glowed.

"I'm not peeping if that's what you think."

"Nope! I never thought that."

"Our after-supper-stroll ended too abruptly in my opinion. I'm just mulling over how it got cut short. I don't know much about the art of courting, Mr. Blake."

John exhaled with a rush of amused breath. "Well Ruby Red doesn't either. It won't take much sparking to set her running in retreat until she warms up to it. You'll get it figured out. You strike me as a man who gets what he goes after.

"Her nightmares and headaches are back since you two had your run-in. They're not bad like when she was younger, but she's definitely stirred up. She's put off dealing with her memories far too long. It's time she gets herself straight and moves away from them. It could be, Marcus, that you are the best way for her to heal."

Both men stood silently for a while and as if in chorus shook their heads slightly and walked away from each other in different directions.

## CHAPTER

## CHAPTER 29

Jake James sat all alone at a greasy table in a back corner of the Jersey Lilly Saloon. His jaw was cradled in place by a soiled bandana tied around his head. The whipping he'd taken from Marcus Dobbs had taken a toll. His face still throbbed in pain. His innards felt scrambled and were spotting his drawers. He had been unconscious when Triple B hands unloaded him from the wagon and carried him into the quack doctor's office at Langtry.

Dobbs had broken Jake's jaw in two places and a bone in his eye socket was cracked. He'd lost some teeth. The combined aching and drainage from the accumulation of injuries was dreadful. His condition was all-consuming.

Nothing was healing quickly or correctly. Dobbs had landed in his middle with the force of a steam engine going full throttle. The blow had churned his guts and caused him to spit blood. Most tiresome was the dark watery dribble he had to contend with from the other end. It had slowed somewhat but a foul stench hung in the air around him. Not even the soiled doves would accept his money in exchange for conversation. For the time being Jake was doomed to isolation giving him plenty of time to plot revenge.

The quack claimed his bowels were bruised and promised that his condition would get slowly better or worse. He couldn't chew well enough to tolerate solid foods. He was living on broth, beer and laudanum. His mind was fettered with the poison of hatred which manifested itself like an illness. He was driven by an obsession to take Ruby back as his. Even in this shape he was cunning at manipulating. He was scheming a way for them to marry and cement the woman to him.

Blake's men had been blind-sided by the vile nastiness of vicious words, obscenities and the nasty accusations Jake hurled against Ruby in the bunkhouse. None of them cared for James and collectively thought him to be worthless. His sleazy demeanor had earned him suspicion and he'd nary a friend on the ranch. There was no solid cvidcncc that he was up to no good but that had been the general consensus. If it had been deduced that he had designs on Miss Ruby he'd have been jumped before this, but he'd not given a hint.

IIe had danccd with hcr once at the roundup social and had come close to blowing his cover then. He recalled Ruby tensing with alarm, but her hero had cut in before anyone else noticed.

How stupid it had been for him to voice those unsolicited, slanderous words in the bunkhouse! That had been his downfall. Jake had listened to the men teasing Dobbs that morning at breakfast just before the fight. It sounded like they all considered Ruby to be Marcus's girl and the green-eyed monster of jealousy had colored his judgement.

It was hard to wrap his head around what had taken place the day before. Marcus had stayed silently disengaged taking the brotherly ribbing in stride. It was clear that everyone approved the idea of Ruby and him being a couple. They were celebrating Marcus's good fortune. The party-like atmosphere became more than Jake could tolerate and he'd exploded!

His uncouth insults had been an unwise attempt to make Ruby seem undesirable as a bride to Dobbs. It had instead earned him the beating of his life. The cowboy rushed to defend her honor.

Jake's mental state had been deteriorating rapidly ever since fed by pain, anger and laudanum. His grasp on reality had slipped to a bizarre level and his brain's abstract reasoning wasn't based on rational thinking. He had literally become a predator. His incomprehensible persona had been buried for so long. Once it was unleashed, he could no longer contain it. His present mental state was most dangerous. His type of insanity was deadly.

In James's frame of mind Ruby Blake was his property. His gangrenous thoughts convinced him that she lusted after his affections and that she'd been taken by Dobbs against her will. He had detailed fantasies of her night and day. He imagined her as his willing love slave. In vivid hallucinations she met all of his desires and satisfied all of his wanton needs.

Until Marcus Dobbs arrived at the ranch, Jake's delusions had lived in the back of his brain with no immediate action required. That had started changing once he realized Ruby and the cowboy were friendly. When Dobbs publicly claimed Ruby for his own Jake's rage burst forth. The kindling of Jake's anger sparked into flames with the comradery in the bunk house. The bitter pill Jake was forced to swallow set a ticking time bomb between his ears that grew louder. He wanted to strangle the suitor and had tried to discourage Marcus's desires by testifying to Ruby's dishonorable character.

In hysterical fury he'd bellowed that she was no better than the worst of the doves who cooed at the filthiest saloon halls. He had shouted countless obscene statements degrading her name. Once the words started, he became powerless to stop the nastiness from spewing forth. Dobbs had beaten the hell out of him in retaliation.

His outbursts had ended up costing him his advantage of invisibility for the moment, but he would take control again. His total possession of Ruby Blake was coming soon. Jake intended to take his woman back and kill Dobbs like he should have done in the first place.

In desperation Jake had gotten word to his older brother who was the cruelest man he knew. He was a back-shooter and rustler who ran a gang of bandit cut throats willing to back up his conscious-less activities. With his brother on board to rustle Blake's herd half-way to market he'd have an opportunity to grab Ruby back. First, he had to force Blake to resort to a cattle drive over land instead of the rancher's plans to ship them on the rails.

Remembering everything the foreman said about the railway stock wagons ordered to pick up the herd had given James a brilliant idea. He'd been brooding out the details of the scheme that would force the rich, high and mighty John Blake to reroute his cattle on the hoof through open country. It would give his brother and the gang easy access to them and make it possible to grab Ruby in the confusion.

Tomorrow he was sending an illiterate drifter to a neighboring town with a message he'd written. The dumb poke would never be the wiser that he was sending a telegram canceling the Triple B's order for rail wagons. He'd put Blake's name to it and if anyone questioned the rider's authority, he'd be instructed to say that he rides for the Triple B outfit. He'd say that he'd been directed by John Blake to send the telegram. Jake would pay the bum and have him ride out from there and never come back this way.

He couldn't risk sending a telegram from Langtry himself. Blake would be given a heads-up. This way the man would be shit-out-of-luck by the time he realized no stock cars were coming for his cattle. He would have to resort to a quickly thrown together cattle drive. With a bit of luck, Ruby, Dobbs and the cattle would be set up for easy pickings on the trail. A lot could happen between here and their destination. Jake would let his brother manage the rest of the details.

There would be many opportunities to shoot Marcus Dobbs and grab Ruby. There was no doubt about that. He would snatch Ruby and Dobbs would die. His brother would be satisfied to take Blake's fat herd for his trouble.

# CHAPTER 30

The Triple B round up had drawn to a successful close many weeks ago with the annual community celebration to mark the end of it. The new calves were counted, branded and turned out to pasture with their mamas. The high-blooded breeding bulls had been redistributed among the several remaining herds. The yearlings that were intended for market this year were contained and guarded in a big expanse of acreage closer to ranch headquarters. This grass had been saved specifically to provide rich grazing for the cattle while waiting for shipment. Blake would be shipping close to twenty-two hundred head as soon after July the Fourth as the railroad could get the cars he'd ordered to Langtry. The cars were in high demand this time of year and there was a waiting list for the ranchers who did not sign up in time to get on the first list. John Blake had thrown his hat into the ring long ago for the cattle freight wagons. He was confident that everything was all set and he was resting easy.

The Independence Day celebration for the neighboring ranches had been planned for weeks. A beef would be barbecued, and all would bring food to share like they'd done after the round up for years. There would be homemade ice cream, a much livelier dance than the last get together, games and fireworks. Many would bring their wagons and bedrolls to camp around the ranch place before leaving out the next morning. A hearty breakfast would be cooked outdoors for all who stayed overnight.

Ruby found herself in a most light-hearted mood as preparations for Independence Day were in progress. Her mustangs were right on schedule with the addition of Marcus's experienced help. He was such an asset to her operation. She hoped to have the newly broken mounts ready soon after the hands drove the herd into Langtry for shipment.

Today she was working happily with Jess, Mary Jane and Cook. They were busy baking loaves of buttery bread, pans of cinnamon rolls, chocolate cakes and fruit pies for the picnic. Ruby and Mary Jane had gleaned the kitchen garden of the first fresh vegetables ready to harvest. She had snapped beans by the hour and made gallons of lemonade now stored in the cool cellar. The rest of the food was ready too. The hands had set up plank tables, benches, and tarps for the shade that would be welcomed in the heat.

By 10:00 AM the crowd started arriving. The big meal would be set out later in the afternoon. In the meantime, slices of bread were ready for quick sandwiches of preserves and butter to hold people over. There was a drink table with hot coffee, milk, buttermilk and cool water to wash it down. The lemonade would be saved for the dance.

The cowboys were in high, celebratory spirits. They had done an extra heap of hard toil for several weeks straight and they could kick back now. This festive reprieve from summer work would be a good way to blow off steam and a chance to make some noise with their guns. Hopefully not long after the shindig they would receive the go-ahead to drive the cattle and hold them just outside of Langtry. That would put them in closer proximity to be loaded on the rail.

They might have to hold them near the town for a few days and they were looking forward to the camping and trail drive atmosphere. Cook had already loaded the chuck wagon and was mostly ready to leave ahead of the herd at a moment's notice. Since the bunkhouse cook would be gone for a few days Mary Jane and Jess would feed those left to do the routine ranch work.

The outdoor dance floor was full of clomping feet and already rowdy in a most good-humored way. Lots of music, noise and boisterous thumping sounded on the plank boards telling of the high time all were having. Everyone had eaten their fill at least twice and most young and old were dancing and laughing it off. Ruby was helping serve lemonade at the drink table. Hands or neighbors had asked her for dances often. She had to admit to herself that she was having a fine time even if she had been keeping an eye out especially for Marcus. He had not yet asked her to dance. She told herself that he was only a curiosity and nothing more. She tried to convince herself that she really didn't care one way or the other if he made an effort to dance with her.

Uncle John pulled her to the dance floor and had her spinning like a top and breathless. He hadn't pushed his niece any more about the courtship he'd set in motion. She was relieved that he had dropped the discussion but there was no doubt that it was still on the table and expected. He had made it perfectly clear that he refused to believe or consider her claims of not being interested in Marcus other than his expertise with horses.

She was lost in self-searching thoughts when the very man she had been looking for previously cut in on a turn to claim her. Uncle John swiftly relinquished her into his arms without breaking the rhythm of the reel and melted away.

Taking John's playful wink as a cue Marcus whipped

Ruby Red away with a flourish of exaggeration without missing a beat. The smooth motion of it made her laugh out loud and then giggle. It was a frivolous sound coming from a mostly somber girl and it was like a cool drink on a hot day to Marcus. Neither of them spoiled the moment with unnecessary words. He deftly steered her around at such a fast pace that they both had soon lost their breaths. Ruby put her hand on her chest gasping for air. It was easy for her to be happy when she was being swept away at this speed in the strong muscled arms of the most handsome man she had ever met. She was coming to depend on him for companionship more and more.

The song came to an end all too quickly and she started to step back as she thought she should, but he held her firmly around the waist waiting for the music to begin again. She tried to look away from his stare but found that she couldn't. Their eyes locked together for a moment and held. Feeling self-conscious she dropped her lashes and secreted a look up through them. The scar above his eyebrow and the greenish bruise under his eye were still faintly evident. Maybe he would always carry the mark where Jess had put the stitches. She wondered not for the first time if he might always remember that it was because of her he wore it. The possibility of him forgetting turned her suddenly melancholy for she knew without a doubt the memory of his heroics would always stay with her.

Thankfully a new dance began, and he gathered her close to his chest. She could feel the rising and falling of his breathing on her cheek and hear the thumping of his heart. She had never felt so peaceful, safe and comforted. He kept her close for the next two waltzes. She savored his manly scent and the puffs of his breath on her hair. She was branded by the slight pressure of his body against hers as they glided around and around the floor. The pleasure of it was making her heady. Finally, he guided her by the elbow to the punch table. With full cups in hand he walked her toward the back of the ranch house away from prying eyes. He saw her seated on a log and then took a seat by her. They sipped the sweet refreshing liquid and looked up into the clear sky. The stars were just beginning to come out.

"It seems we'll soon have the mustangs finished. The number left is dwindling down fast," he observed. "Does this mean that you soon won't need me?"

She responded with feigned indignation, "Have you forgotten so easily that you're still in my custody?"

"No, Ma'am! I just thought that you might not need me in the stables anymore."

"The Mesteneros and his son are already gathering a new herd for me. They'll run them in sometime after the cattle get off to market. As soon as things settle down around here, you'll be busy enough with the new horses. Besides, you always have a job here on the Triple B in the stables for as long as you want it."

"That's a mighty tempting offer, Sunshine Girl. A man could get used to this place. It's the first time I've felt at home since–well, in a long time. I truly do love the wrangling and working alongside you and Blue John. It's always been my dream to raise and train horses. However, I've always had a hankering to be my own boss. Working for a sassy girl like you has never been a specific goal of mine."

Ruby smiled. She was warmed from the inside out by hearing him speak the nickname he used for her. It brought on a distinctive feeling that sharpened a fidgety awareness that she had come to look forward to feeling.

"Why do you call me that sometimes?"

Without warning Marcus flashed his most dazzling smile at her and winked. "What, Sunshine Girl or sassy?"

Taking on a teasing, cavalier Texas twang he continued. "Sunshine Girl is for that hair of yours, Ruby Red. It's as yellow as the sun! The name suits you just fine. Sassy is for that smart mouth of yours which I must admit gives you a certain annoying charm."

"You're teasing me, Marcus! What a smooth-talking devil you are! Still, I am getting a little too used to sweet-talk, cowboy. It's making me soft. Remember I'm only tolerating your attention until this notion of you and me courting blows over. I don't need you as a beau, Marcus. I don't need anyone to get close. I've been doing just fine by myself. Let's just pretend to court when someone is looking like we agreed. We're just doing this to satisfy Uncle John. It's best that neither of us forget what we're doing."

"You're so mistaken, little cowgirl. You don't have it figured out that you can't hide any longer, do you? Your uncle, who loves you beyond reason, is trying to take better care of you than you take of yourself. He knows that life changes and with it, we change too. It's time to let the past rest and give yourself some peace in the now, Ruby!

"Even Jess is worried about what's to become of you if you don't start living for today and tomorrow instead of in the past with old hurts. You've been avoiding reality, Ruby. You think you're safe behind ranching, guns and horses. You've spent your emotions on shooting targets and hiding in trees!

"Yes! Jess is so bothered about you that he told me where you were the evening I couldn't find you! Crying your heart out in a tree so that no one could see you? Don't hide from me anymore. I can see you even when I can't! Lean on me–take a rest. You must be exhausted from keeping it together all on your own. I get worn out just watching you struggle sometimes."

"Are you done, Mr. Dobbs?"

"Pretty much! How mad are you, Miss Ruby?"

He reached out and curled his fingers under her chin and gently outlined her bottom lip with his thumb. "Now, honey, there goes that little, pouty lip again. I've warned you about that once already." At this he tapped her bottom lip twice, teasing it with his index finger. He paused in contemplation and then withdrew his touch. "Come on. Let's dance some more. It's getting late and the fireworks will start soon."

Glad to escape, she rose to head back the way they'd come. He caught her by the waist and turned her around in an arced circle that lifted her feet clear off the ground. She couldn't help but let out a squeal at the suddenness of it.

"No!" Marcus corrected. "We'll dance right now–right here–right under the stars. This is our time and place! We can make our own music together just fine."

He took her in strong arms and waltzed her around in the grass keeping time with his heart. He even dipped her and she giggled so he dipped her again just to hear his favorite melody once more.

They joined the celebration at the tank to watch the fireworks. There had to be an ever-watchful vigilance in case the showers of light sparked a fire. This spot by the tank was chosen for the ready supply of water that it afforded. Buckets, blankets and men with horses were readied as a precaution.

Marcus and Ruby stood together. Their necks craned in unison to see the beautiful colors launched high in the sky to fall back to earth in shattered falls. The bright bursts seemed to hang momentarily at their highest point before descending softly. Each cracking eruption was followed by ooohs and ahhhhs from the gathered crowd. The back of Marcus's hand brushed hers. He made no grab for possession, but he reached out with one finger to stroke the back of her fingers. He was gratified by her quiet acceptance. She did not shy at this small offering of an intimate touch. Had he known of the pattering it caused in her chest he might have risked more.

The crowd clapped and cheered dispersing at the end of

the show to their settling places for the night. Young children rested their heads on their fathers' shoulders. It was a cozy sight.

Marcus took Ruby's elbow and walked her slowly to the ranch house door. She turned to face him before going in and he leaned one arm against the door facing. He bent slightly to hover closely over her for a moment.

"Thank you, Marcus," she said sincerely as she tilted her head up to meet his gaze.

"For what exactly, sunshine? You thank me for what?"

"Thank you for dancing with me, for talking, for walking, for the fireworks and for being honest with me. Thank you for not pushing me. You've made this the best Fourth of July of my life. I'm not used to being escorted to a party."

"Ruby, I can't imagine why a pretty girl like you would ever be without beaus. You look lovely in a handsome dress and the way you wear it is thought provoking. You look beautiful. It's enough to drive a weaker man crazy, hon."

"You don't have to pretend with me any longer. It's just the two of us alone now. I can talk Uncle John out of pushing me off onto you. Truly, it is okay. I understand that I'm not like a regular girl. We both know it, Marcus.

"No man chooses to spend time with a female who can outshoot, out rope and out ride them. I don't think that I can change and be something more or less than I am. Uncle John will just have to accept the facts as they are."

"Whoa! You're right about only one thing. You certainly aren't like any standard, starchy, uptight female who I've ever known. Rest assured though that I like you just the way you are. You don't have to change for me and I'm willing to work on that sassy little mouth that gets you into so much trouble!

"To be perfectly honest I do like your confidence and spunk. Make no mistake, woman, I spent time with you this evening because I wanted to make time with the prettiest girl here. This time is nothing about trying to please your uncle.

"Oh, and one other thing! You're taking a lot for granted, little girl. Where did you get the idea that I can't out shoot, out rope and out ride you? We'll just have to see about that!" He winked.

"I never once thought or said you couldn't. I was talking about other men in general." She turned to go inside.

"Ruby," he whispered, touching her arm lightly.

She turned and almost bumped into him. He had stepped into her space. "What? What, Marcus?"

How he longed to give her a soft kiss, hold her in his arms and nuzzle her neck! It was all he could do to keep his arms from reaching out and pulling her in. "Have you ever been kissed by a man?"

"No, Marcus."

"I didn't think so.

"I'll help you with that load of grief you're carrying, Ruby. You just wait and see if I don't. Goodnight, Ruby." He smiled a big, winning smile, tipped his hat in a most gallant fashion and winked at her like a rogue.

She was so thirsty for his attentions that his actions caused a trill like a musical scale to run through her body. She returned the sweet smile, "Goodnight, cowboy."

She stepped into the house closing the door behind her and leaned against it. He had called her pretty again. That's what she'd heard, and the compliment filled her mind like sparkles from the fireworks. The sparks were hanging overhead and showering down.

She had no idea that he was leaning against the other side of the door. The fireworks were exploding in his chest and not above.

# CHAPTER 31

With the Independence Day festivities officially over the next morning guests started moving out. Whiskey passed out in a deep sleep on the porch. Pete sidled up to John as they waved their neighbors off.

"Boss, we need to talk."

"Let's go to my office then."

Once the door was closed, he poured Pete and himself two fingers of amber whiskey. "You sound like something's wrong, Pete. What is it?"

"I don't rightly know for sure if anything is wrong, but I think I should pass some information along."

"Okay–it's early to be drinking but I feel like it. We deserve it after hosting such a fine celebration, I reckon. Now, tell me what you want me to know."

Some of the hands from the other spreads were talkin' yesterday. Word is getting around as words have a way of doin'. It's being said that one of the Triple B hands is in Langtry shooting his mouth off about getting even with you and Marcus. It's easy to guess that it's Jake James. He's no doubt disgruntled over the hammering he took from Marcus and being fired by you. Ruby's name hasn't been brought up the best I can tell.

"It's also bein' said that he looks and acts to be ailing. He always was a man of weak pallor. To hear it now he's noticeably thinner, yellow-looking and sicklier. His face is ruined and has to be kept wrapped in a cloth just to keep it together. He's suffering misery from the beatin'. The Langtry quack didn't help him none.

"I'm thinkin' one of us needs to have a talk with Marcus about keeping an eye out for trouble. I'm thinkin' both of you need to stay armed and alert until this thing blows over.

"Here's the kicker that slipped by all of us! This Jake James is Trank James's little brother. Who would have thought that? I sure never made the connection."

John let out a low, drawn out whistle. "That's a damn revelation just now coming to light and a risky complication! Jake James may be festering for a retribution."

"That's exactly what I'm thinkin' too, Boss."

Frank James terrorized Texas with a gang of misfit Mexicans who still wanted to live as bandits. They raided, stole, burned and killed. The idea of the notorious outlaw and his criminal band having any kind of link to the Triple B was dangerous. The man was a cold-bloodied killer without a conscience. Stealing, dealing havoc and inflicting pain left a trail the Texas Rangers had only been able to follow. The reward on Trank's head was hefty but bounty hunters stayed clear of him. He was a cunning and dangerous desperado.

"You're right, Pete, Marcus needs this information straightaway. I don't want Ruby gettin' hold of it though.

She's always believed she'd have to face outlaws riding in one day. I don't want to feed her dread by sounding an alarm!

"Tell the hands to be on guard for signs of trouble of any kind and to stay armed. Tell them if they notice anything out of the ordinary, small or large, to report to you or me immediately. Don't tell too many details yet. There's no use inciting panic until it's necessary. I hope we're just borrowing trouble, but I don't have a good feeling about this.

"Since you're here, Pete, there's another problem to talk over. This is a worrisome situation! I've not received any word from the railroad about when to expect the cattle wagons I ordered to be moved into Langtry. I was planning on having an idea by now so we could go ahead and drive the herd into a holding position outside of town. I was expecting to be notified by now of when the railroad would have the stock wagons here.

"Yet each day passes without word! Jonson's T-Bow brand got the go ahead two days ago. Now, I know for sure that I filed before Jonson. Let's take a ride into town and check this out. Pete, something's wrong. I can feel it in my bones."

"Sure seems like when it rains it pours! Maybe there's just been an explainable mix-up of some kind," Pete commiserated.

John Blake's inquiry into the railroad's schedule snowballed into an epic snowstorm of blizzard proportions! He sent a wire to find out where and why the Triple B stock wagons were being held up. A quick return wire from the railroad specified that the directive had been received by his earlier wire to cancel the order. Available cars were subsequently rerouted to others on the waiting list. At this time none were in route marked for the Triple B.

Blake threw his hat on the ground and wadded up the

paper. He fired back a telegram asking for more information exposing who sent the instructions to cancel his order. He also told the railroad to send his loading cars.

Smoke came out of his ears when the telegram fired back that his name would be put on the bottom of the list per railroad protocol. Many ranchers were in line ahead of him now. He'd forfeit the price advantage of being among the first to market and the loss would be considerable. Blake couldn't afford to waste time and energy on being angry about something that he couldn't change. That luxury would have to be put on the back burner until later, and indeed, he planned to get to the bottom of where the cancelation originated. There would be hell to pay.

Strong emotions wouldn't get his beef cattle to market or put money in his pocket. He needed them on the way as soon as possible before the market softened. The cash they'd bring was needed for operating expenses throughout the coming year. At their present weight and condition, he was hoping for at least thirty-five dollars to forty dollars a head. If he didn't get them moving now the profits would shrink substantially. This unforeseen development forced him to throw different plans together in a hurry and he could think of only one thing to do.

Back at the ranch with Pete, Jess, Marcus, Ruby and Bowie crowded into his office, John laid the glitch out for all to hear. Whiskey was curled up on a rag rug snoozing not far from his boy oblivious to the turmoil his people were facing. Blake and Pete started throwing together and outlining a hastily arranged trail drive into Abilene. The buyers, who would ship to Chicago, would be congregating there with their heavy purses.

The herd would have to be driven the two hundred miles through desolate harsh country that was dry, ragged and varmint infested. Lots of perils lay in wait along the way. Ranchers rarely chanced trail drives any longer with the rails being the better, quicker and safer choice.

Together they made a list of those who would go and those hands who would be left behind. A skeleton crew would be assigned to ranch chores and to keep the place secured. John was on full alert for trouble at home but made no mention of it in front of Ruby and Bowie. Old maps from previous cattle drives before the railroad laid track were being studied. Hopefully the water sources marked hadn't dried up and were still adequate.

Jess was commandeered and already busied himself getting the chuck wagon restocked for a long stretch with food and supplies. The gear necessary for the cowboys to be on the move was already being gathered into the hoodlum wagon that would follow the chuck. Everything and every person had to be ready to pull out in no more than a couple of days. Daylight was burning and every hour they delayed increased the tension.

A string of stock horses was cut out for the remuda and three hands were assigned to wrangle horses and tack. One of them would drive the hoodlum wagon carrying gear, bedrolls and extra supplies. Each rider would need at least two fresh mounts a day available. Hands would be in the saddle ten to twelve hours at a stretch and throughout the night. A cowboy could even go through three horses a day.

Blake wanted his fat stock to arrive at market with as much weight on them as possible. The cattle could not be pushed harder than they could tolerate without losing too much. With luck and little trouble, the drive could take around twenty days, more or less. There were always unforeseen hold ups of one sort or another on drives with a herd this size. Managing twenty-two hundred head was an undertaking only seasoned cowboys could handle.

Pressure was running high on the Triple B as preparations took priority over everything else. Drives were nearly a thing of the past. Pete was experienced so would be the ramrod on the drive. The others were made up mostly of veterans with herding experience.

Bowie had never been on a long haul so his uncle and Ruby definitely wanted him to have the experience. Whiskey would tag along with him, but he would be an asset. That meant there was no way to keep Ruby at home, but on the plus side, her expertise would be invaluable.

The evening before the cattle were to head out Blake pulled Marcus aside for a private heart-to-heart. He rehashed the talk in town concerning the disgruntled Jake. Both men were judiciously confident that by the time Marcus returned to the Triple B the miscreant would have calmed down and moved out of the territory. To help ensure this Blake would contact area ranchers to warn them about Jake's unstable character and affiliations. He was going to advise them not to attach trouble to their families or outfits. Not one area rancher would hire a man after a word of warning from the Triple B.

"Marcus, on a strictly personal level, please watch out for my children for me. Ruby thinks she's totally self-sufficient and she is to a point but she's not above making a mistake. She's also a beautiful young woman who needs looking after by a man even if she disagrees. I know that she'll keep track of Bowie every step of the way and Whiskey is fiercely protective of him. Since I'm not going to be there, I'll rest easier knowing that you'll do your best by them.

"Jess will be on the chuck wagon and no doubt he'll let you know if he thinks things aren't going right. I told him that I'd be talking to you. Pete will be watching too but he'll have his hands full enough. His attentions will be spread thin."

"You don't even have to ask. I was planning on doing it already, Boss. I'll guard them with my life." The determined look on Marcus's face told Blake that he meant it.

"Could it be that you have feelings for our bona fide cowgirl?" asked John, expectantly.

"I do, but affectionate feelings have to run both ways to count. It's a might early to say if your marriage blackmail will be successful. I will tell you this, though. She interests me like no other woman. We'll just have to wait and see. She's guarded–not one to admit to anything easily–but yes, I have some feelings for her."

"Don't let Ruby know that we've made a protection pact between us. She'd likely avoid you the whole trip. I wouldn't put it past her even to make it hard for you. Your chances for any sparking after that would be diminished to nothing."

"Boss, I have a feeling they're slim to almost none anyway," laughed Marcus. "She's as skittish as a young colt and I'm having to take things real slow with her."

The two men nodded with knowing looks. "We better head to bed, Marcus. Jess will be banging the bell before sunrise. I'll ride out in the morning to see you across the Pecos River. Then I'll return to the ranch.

"I'm planning to take the train into Abilene in a couple of weeks to make the necessary arrangements to sell for the highest price that I can negotiate. I'll be calling on a longtime lady friend. I'm seriously thinking of marriage again after all these years without the comfort of a good woman."

"You old fox!"

"Keep it under your hat for now."

Morning came early with the offensive clamoring of Jess's triangle. Even though the trek ahead promised to be grueling there was enthusiasm in the air as the cowboys readied to pull out. The noise was music to the ears in spite of the perils and challenges that lay ahead. It was a given the herd would probably spook at some point, storms would surely blow, rattlesnakes and varmint holes could be disastrous, and the availability of water was a somber consideration.

There was no need to distress over the worst possible scenarios before they happened, but dangers did exist. Cattle rustlers could set their sights on the herd. Renegade Indians could be waiting for easy spoils. Pete was certainly a capable boss and the men were well-armed, but the cowboys would need to be constantly vigilant. John Blake would pray for safe travels.

He stayed along the bank of the Pecos as the herd crossed over in a long, thin string that stretched out for a couple of miles moving in a line of sorts. He wished the drivers well as they came through with the ones riding drag being the last of them. The wagons had gone first. It was Jess's job to travel ahead and pick the place to bed down overnight and the trail boss's job to keep them on course and schedule.

Blake sat at the river on his horse until he could no longer hear the cracking whips, the whistles, the bawling, the clacking of hooves and horns or Whiskey's occasional barking. Since Ruby, Bowie and Marcus were riding flank today, he'd had time to bid them a final farewell. He was gratified they were on good horses as he turned his horse in the direction of home.

His life would feel empty while they were away but for the next two weeks, he'd be busy nailing down the ranch against any assault Trank James might rain down upon the Triple B.

He was determined to get answers about the canceled rail cars. He had to know who had stopped the delivery of those cars and why. Tomorrow, he would start digging into that mystery with a fine-toothed comb. He'd get to the bottom of the mystery. He finally had time to allow himself to feel anger over the interference.

The solitude would also allow him to think about Laura

and their future together. He'd recently received a letter from her, and she remained unmarried. He was going to ask her to marry him. The dynamics of his little family was changing, and he needed to make adjustments too.

Seeing Ruby and Marcus skirting around the issues of being a couple had caused him to ponder on his reasons for putting off his own desires. The arguments he'd always found so valid for staying single had dwindled considerably. He wondered what Ruby and Bowie would think about him marrying after all these years, but he was forty-three and still felt the stirrings of passion.

He and Mary Jane would rattle around the place for the next few weeks. Mary Jane had plans of a big spring cleaning in both the ranch house and her cabin and had banished him to the bunkhouse for meals which suited him fine. He'd promised Ruby that he would check on Blue John in the stable. They both trusted Blue John to stay on top of things but their old friend might need something.

Jess located a place to bed down the cattle for the night with a grove of trees to shelter the camp. Pete had not intended to make more than a few miles this afternoon after getting the herd across the Pecos. This evening would be a fun night in camp with tomorrow starting the real push. Men had to be stationed with the herd around the clock. Night watch could be handled with three rotations of six hands each. During the days the position of the drivers would be rotated so no one would eat the worst of the dust all the time. Riding drag was the very dirtiest assignment and the drovers would all pull that duty equally.

# CHAPTER 32

A fter several days on the trail routines were established. Each morning started with a hearty breakfast of biscuits, flapjacks or whatever Jess chose to make. Before heading out for the day, each hand would wrap up a share of the leavings and stow them in saddlebags for a quick midday meal to be washed down with water from canteens. By supper time, the boys would be tired, dirty and plenty ready to eat a hot meal. Whiskey begged for bites, bones and pets.

Cows would be butchered along the way for fresh meat as needed. They also butchered out any falling with broken legs or other injuries. There were cured hams, tinned meats, cooking staples, syrup, and dried fruits in the cook's larder. Two milk cows were tied to the hoodlum wagon. Eggs were packed in the flour and any time they came close to settlers they bargained for more eggs.

Each day was a slow-go allowing the herd to graze and rest at times. They could not be pushed too hard and maintain their monetary value. After supper most drivers were ready to hit the hay especially if they were on night watch rotation. At night the cattle were herded into a bunch for security.

Cowboys slept with one eye open and could be ready in a snap to leave their bedrolls at the slightest hint of tension. It was not impossible for a cowboy to work two to three days in a row without rest if unforeseen circumstances warranted it.

A week into the drive, things had been running smoothly. Spirits were running high. Possibly the cowboys were becoming careless since the time had gone so quietly without incident. Marcus was good to his word and kept a close watch on Ruby and the boy without being obvious.

She returned to camp each day looking disheveled and tired to the bone, but never once did she complain. Usually right after chow, she'd put her bedroll under Jess's wagon and go to sleep.

Bowie looked worn out too but he would try to stay up as long as the wild stories were being passed around. Whiskey would lie beside him snoring. Marcus couldn't blame Bowie for wanting to hear the yarns of past drives, shootouts and days gone by. The embellishments of the storytellers were priceless and most often bigger than life.

This day they had stopped early due to finding a stream of water that was too good to pass up. Pete decided to give the men and cattle a rest and even leave out a little later than usual the next morning. They all needed to clean up and wash a few clothes. Most were caked with sweat and grime. Everyone would either bathe of their own volition or be boisterously thrown in the water by friends. The cattle would be given the chance for all the water they could hold.

The cowboys waded into the water in small groups as soon as they were released from herd duty. Digressing to childish banter, they dunked, splashed and hollered good-naturedly. Ruby stayed with the herd as the cowboys left in shifts to bathe and wash out belongings. Her turn would come after supper when they'd be finished, and she could have the privacy she needed.

Jess had passed the word that the drovers would finish with their washing and ablutions before chow time. After supper no man would be allowed down by the stream. No one could wander from camp at that time except to return to the herd for duty.

Ruby slipped off quietly with her saddle bags of dirty clothes, soft towel from home and the perfumed soap she favored. Her hair had lost its sheen under layers of trail dust worked all the way to her scalp. It was heavy and odorous with days of accumulated sweat.

She was confident that no one followed her. Jess had guaranteed the uninterrupted time for bathing. She took her time unbraiding her hair and running her fingers through the strands. Her shirt and pants were peeled off slowly and added to the wash pile. She sat lazily in the grass and stretched her legs, pointing her toes out and moaning. She stretched her arms and held them suspended above her head in the air. A little squeal escaped with the delightful feeling of freedom.

Ruby stood and shed her lacey chemise and then untied the ruffled drawers letting them puddle around her feet. From one side of the saddle bags she retrieved the bar of soap, the towel and the extra set of clean clothes. She lay them beside the water and waded slowly into the stream with the soap.

Marcus cautiously followed Ruby to the stream keeping out of sight and unheard. He was acting as a guard but that wasn't entirely true. He was curious. He'd thought of her bathing all day and had been riding herd with an arousal most of the afternoon.

When he stopped near the place Ruby had chosen, he slipped in a little closer for a better vantage point. The first glimpse of the beautiful girl in the thin, feminine under clothes confirmed that he was officially and hopelessly besotted. The image of her tightly stretching extremities and the creamy, soft-looking skin slammed his manhood with a jolt! He knew without a doubt that he'd never been this aroused before.

She stood and took the bottom edge of her chemise in her hands and slowly stripped it off her body. The lush firm breasts with rosy, pebbled nipples were fit for an angel's head to rest.

*Lord have mercy, woman! You can be my girl!*

A river of heated blood coursed through his body in anticipation as she pulled the drawstring at her waist and the drawers dropped to the ground. She stood there in all her glory. There wasn't an undesirable place on Ruby's body. Luscious, ample curves graced every good place known to man.

He held his breath as she soaped up and dunked herself just to repeat the process. His mouth watered and then it would grow dry only to moisten up again.

*Have mercy–Ruby, you're killing me slowly!*

Coherent thoughts escaped him, and the fabric of his pants was stretched beyond the limit of endurance. He felt inspired like a young buck with his first doe. Marcus couldn't risk being caught in his indiscretion. He slipped away and cautiously made his way back to camp.

He was in camp when Ruby got back and was innocently settled into a card game with a couple of the boys. His faked concentration on the game made him appear totally unaware of her arrival. He wasn't about to do anything to garner suspicion.

Marcus didn't acknowledge her return as he had no intent of facing her right now. There was no reason she'd have to be suspicious of him trespassing but guilt on his face might give him away.

*Jess if you only knew about the breach in your security, you'd shoot me.* My grave would be dug right out here in the middle of nowhere and I'd be buried.

The accountability of his actions and what he deserved was foremost on his mind. The opportunity he had taken was stolen pleasure. He did think it ironic that he and Ruby had both spied on each other.

He felt sheepish at the memories of Ruby soaking. They played havoc with parts of his body that interfered with sleeping the night. The only flimsy defense for taking advantage this afternoon was that she played the game first.

That very moment he decided to respectfully marry Ruby as soon as possible. He'd truly compromised her as John Blake had once accused him. Marcus's pa had raised a gentleman.

A small measure of punishment came to Marcus when it was time to get up the next morning because he'd hardly slept. His rashness had plagued him all night. He was also tormented by how her shiny yellow hair sparkled in the light from the fire. He filled his plate and sat a distance away. He got real busy eating when she came over to sit by him. Never had food held his interest as it did now.

It was Ruby's turn to ride drag with a couple of others today. She wrapped her freshly washed hair up in a bandana and tucked it all under her hat to keep it clean. The turquoise on her hat band and the light blue bandanna peeking from under her hat were striking together. Even looking at her all covered up against the onslaught of dust made Marcus feel edgy again. A detailed copy of her nakedness would forever be etched on the back of his eyelids.

Once the boys started moving the herd out Marcus was

separated from Ruby for the day. He would be working with Bowie on point and they would remain together. Ruby would be at least a mile and a half or more back. Marcus was glad for the distance between them. He needed time to clear his head. Pete would probably stop a little later than usual today since they had waited until ten o'clock to get started. Marcus would send Bowie back to check on his sister in the afternoon.

Bowie rode tall in the saddle and was becoming an accomplished drover. His sister had taught him well in the skills needed to be a good cowboy. He had grown above average for his age and his muscles were developed from hard ranch work. He was a fine healthy specimen of a country boy. His quickness to learn and please made him a damn good hand. He was pulling his own weight on the drive. He was a natural and the cowboys sincerely liked him. Ruby had raised him well regardless of what it had cost her.

After eating cold sausages rolled up in breakfast flapjacks, Marcus took a long swig on his canteen and poured some cool water down the back of his neck in an effort to refresh himself. He'd been unable to quit thinking about Ruby and he'd decided to quit fighting it. He was unsure as to how he would sell her on the notion of marrying him. He hadn't even kissed her yet. There was a reason he'd been waiting to kiss those sweet virgin lips, but the time was at hand.

He'd have to be real careful helping her get past the scary parts of being intimate romantically. He'd be patient so they could have the kind of marriage he wanted but the girl needed to be kissed like a woman by a real man and soon. He'd show her it didn't mean she had to give up her independence.

He was jerked out of his wool gathering by the noise of a drover riding hell bent for leather directly toward him.

"Something's happened to Ruby! Ruby's missing!" he

yelled at Marcus over the noise of the herd. "Pete said I'd better come get you."

"Is she on Big River?" Marcus hoped.

"No, she's on Kingfish."

"Kingfish! Kingfish! Well, I'll be damned! That horse is loco! He's been skittish and unpredictable this whole trip. I should have put a gun to his head! Dammit to hell, what was she doing on him?" demanded Marcus in anger.

"Who knows why Ruby does anything? Trying to ride him out, I guess," the equally frustrated cowboy shook his head.

Marcus did not wait for further explanation. Reassigning the messenger to ride point in his place he galloped off. He waved for Bowie to follow. The two headed out to the end of the herd which turned out to be almost two miles back. From there they were sent even farther back to where she'd last been seen. A rider met them shouting that shots had been fired to the west.

Marcus and Bowie spurred their already lathered mounts and took off in a frenzy of dust finding Pete just as he reached her himself. He was first on the ground with Ruby who was partially trapped beneath the weight of Kingfish. Kingfish was in shock and suffering dreadfully with a broken leg. The horse's eyes were glazed and unseeing. He was snorting snot with his lips peeled back off dry teeth held apart by his extended and rapidly swelling tongue. He needed to be stilled immediately to avoid causing Ruby further injury and to be put out of his misery.

Marcus and Bowie were both off their mounts before their horses came to a full stop. She was barely conscious, but her gun was still in her hand at the end of her outstretched arm. It was pointing to the two dead rattlers dangerously close. They were still nervously twitching from the lingering impulses of failing nerves. Marcus kicked them away in disgust, regret and total frustration.

Pete dispensed an accurate shot to the horse's head

stilling Kingfish instantly and releasing the hellion from further torment. Total fear and shock were registered on Bowie's face as he took in the scene. Perspiration had popped out all over him in anxiety for his sister. Marcus kneeled with Pete who was trying to determine her condition.

The cowboy who'd ridden with Pete and Bowie secured ropes as quickly as possible onto Kingfish and attached them to their horses. He and Bowie backed them up slowly to allow Pete and Marcus to carefully extract Ruby from under the dead weight. Being useful helped Bowie get a handle on his raw emotions and settled him somewhat.

Marcus stroked her paled face with a bandana moistened in canteen water. He kneaded her hand lovingly and called her name but received minimal response. It was at that moment that he truly understood how much he loved her. He used all of his self-control to keep from crying out in helpless anguish over her injuries.

Marcus set about feeling every inch of her looking for damages even though Pete was doing the same thing. She did not appear to have any broken bones which constituted a miracle. There was quite a gash where her head hit a large rock protruding from the ground, and it was bleeding profusely from the swollen area of contact. That was most certainly why she wasn't alert.

Thankfully she'd been at herself long enough to shoot the rattlers before they could strike. They must have spooked the sorry excuse for a horse she was riding.

"Good shot, Ruby. Good shot," Marcus said to her, but she didn't respond.

Momentarily, she stirred but was unable to communicate coherently. Coughing and choking, she turned her head instinctively and retched violently. She weakly moved a hand to her rib cage and moaned. Marcus checked once more. He couldn't feel broken ribs. He opened her shirt lifting up the camisole and saw the deep, purple bruising angrily blooming on both sides of her body. Ruby had passed out again. Marcus took a cloth he used as a towel from his saddle bags and tore strips from it to bind her rib cage and head. The bleeding had subsided to seepage. She obviously needed stitches to close the gash completely and surely, she had a concussion.

A spiral of smoke coiled up into the western horizon. It was most likely from a settler's chimney. A cabin ahead meant help. The cowboys quickly constructed a travois, Indian style, from two scrubby trees and brush. They attached it to Marcus's gelding, Bob. He and Bowie started in the direction of the homestead with an ailing Ruby in tow. The other cowboys collected Kingfish's tack and headed back to the herd. They'd report the accident, Ruby's condition and fill Jess in on the details. Getting her out of the heat and to a place to rest as quickly as possible seemed the wisest thing to do.

Bowie's face was slowly regaining color and he was talking quietly to Whiskey. Other than that, he was sullen as a stone. Marcus's mind was churning with what-ifs. Seeing Ruby so hurt and helpless had thrown his mind into a tizzy. He'd never prayed so hard in all his life. How could he have just discovered how much he loved Ruby Red and she wasn't even conscious so he could tell her? Surely, he'd not have to lose her in the same day he had come to love her.

He tried to sooth Bowie as best he could without letting him know the extent of his own distress. What a blessing Whiskey was such a companion to the boy! Traveling was slow as they tried to keep from jarring Ruby. It took over an hour and a half to get to the edge of the settler's clearing. Marcus had stopped three times to check on his precious cargo. Each time he'd tried to get her to take a few drops of water. He bathed her face and spoke soothing words to her.

They neared the cabin and Marcus called out, "Hello! We have an injured woman."

A white man stepped out of the barn. An Indian woman in typical pioneer clothing and a boy younger than Bowie cautiously stepped out of the cabin door. The woman's hand shaded her eyes against the blazing sun. Marcus dismounted and held out a hand in friendship to the man. His woman and boy did not come forward.

Marcus and the homesteader exchanged words of introduction. It was quickly understood that Marcus's woman was injured and suffering from a riding accident. The man motioned his wife forward. She went straight to the travois, finding Ruby unconscious. She immediately took charge, checking her for injuries again, lifting her eyelids and asking Marcus questions about her accident in English.

The farmer took their horses to the barn to take care of them properly. They had been pushed hard and deserved grain, water and rest. His wife sent the boy to the well for water. Marcus carried Ruby carefully into the family's dwelling and out of the heat. Inside things were neat, orderly and clean. A Bible was open on the table. Something bubbling on the cook stove smelled delicious. This was a Christian home and Marcus praised God for leading them here.

Marcus encouraged Bowie and Whiskey to go to the barn to help with the horses while Ruby was being tended. The tender-hearted boy needed to be spared what was to come. Bowie showed strain from the events on his face and there was no use to add to his stress. Marcus wished he could escape as well but he would not leave Ruby to go through the application of stitches alone.

The gracious woman, whose name was Little Flower, removed the bloody strips wrapped around her head. She examined the deep gash and washed it with the water from the well. She poured whiskey on the cut to clean the wound and ward off infection. Ruby stirred and groaned at the considerable sting.

Little Flower expertly put in seven neat stitches. Marcus held Ruby steady as she was in and out of knowing what was happening. The sutures were painful but thankfully she never fully rallied. She was spared most of the pain and trauma.

Marcus was grim faced and relieved when the sewing was finished. Little Flower applied a thick, healing salve before she bandaged Ruby's head with clean cloth strips that replaced what he had applied earlier to stanch the bleeding. He never wanted so badly to have been the one injured. Ruby had moaned each time the needle went in and came out, but she was never lucid. It was a blessing.

Then she stripped her down to her chemise and drawers. After that she applied a warmed concoction to her severely bruised ribs and wrapped them tightly.

Marcus and Bowie sat with Ruby while the woman went back to her cooking. They would be there for as long as it took for her to gain consciousness. Marcus held her hand while continuing to reassure her little brother in a quiet, calm voice.

"Your sister's looking better–she'll be fine now. You know how tough she is. It will take more than bein' thrown from a horse to do her in."

Little Flower's husband and son came in from the field and ate supper along with Marcus and Bowie. Sometime later Ruby opened her eyes and even kept down a few spoons of willow bark tea and a few spoons of broth. She was confused yet and in pain. Marcus took a small vile of laudanum from his saddle bags and forced Ruby to take a swallow. This gave her relief and she rested again.

She was delirious and disturbed by visions of snakes, the fall and the horse she'd been riding. Marcus squeezed her hand and kissed her cheek several times. He never quit reassuring her that everything would be fine.

"Ruby, you've been hurt. You took a fall. Be still, honey. Bowie and I are right here. It's all good but you need to rest. The snakes are gone. You killed them."

She did not shrink away from his gentle touch and voice. He continued to stroke her forehead and smooth her golden hair back from her face. She was determined to check on Bowie even though he was sitting by the bed. Several times she called out for Marcus. This touched his already tender heart and made him feel even more in love.

"We're both right here–not leaving–close your eyes– we're not leaving."

When she did wake up, she did not stay wakeful for very long throughout the night. It was obvious that her ribs were aching, and her leg was uncomfortable from bruising. She drifted in and out of a restless sleep. Marcus dosed her with laudanum twice more. He was able to lay his head on the bed and lightly doze.

Bowie and his dog went to sleep with the boy in the barn. They'd become quick friends. Bowie could relax and have a break from Ruby's suffering there with his dog and new friend.

Marcus kept vigilance and tended Ruby throughout the night and into the next morning. He was grateful to see improvement and no sign of fever. She was tired but alert and her words were starting to make sense.

"Ruby, Bowie and I have to leave but Little Flower will take care of you so you can recuperate for a couple of days.

"What? I'm going back with you, Marcus. I can't stay here."

"Sure, you can. You're in no condition to ride a horse for a few days. I'll be back to get you before you know it."

"I can ride Big River–I swear–he'll get me back okay."

"Big River isn't here, Ruby Red. Don't you remember? You rode out on Kingfish. I will never understand why you took that crazy horse. He was not fit for anyone to ride. Maybe if you'd been on Big River in the first place none of this would have happened but we'll have that talk later."

"I felt sorry for the horse. Everyone had given up on him. I thought I could iron out the problem. I shouldn't have and now he's dead. I feel terrible about it."

"Well, be that as it may, Bowie and I need to catch up with the herd. Pete's three hands short. I promise you that I'll be back to collect you. Give me a couple of days. I'll get you back to the herd then. I will come back with Big River."

"I really don't want to stay here. I'm telling you to take me with you.

"Tarnation! You are the sassiest female I've ever had to deal with. This is one time you won't be getting your way. Pete needs us. Everyone is waiting on word of how you're doing. We'll be leaving within the hour, Ruby. You can try to get up but you're not going to make it."

"I can get up and I am going back to the herd. I won't stay behind." Ruby tried to lift her torso off the bed but fell back grunting painfully. She clutched her rib cage.

"This place reminds me of the ranch house where Bowie and I came from. It makes me remember things I don't want to think about. I guess you're right about me waiting but don't make me wait any longer than you have to, or I swear you'll be sorry."

"Yes, I don't doubt it will, Ruby, but there's no logic in having you endure riding double on a horse right now. You can't even raise yourself up and you're lightheaded. Get you a couple of days rest. I'll hurry back here and bring Big River with me.

"Pete or I should have put Kingfish down. How foolish it was for you to ride off on him. Your uncle will have both our heads and I don't blame him! I keep thinking about it. Someday you're going to have to face that you're not invincible! It's just lucky you weren't killed this time.

"That loco horse is gone for good. He never settled down even one time on this drive and never would have either. All the boys had quit trying to use him. He'd already thrown one and bitten another. Nobody could have ridden the craziness out of him, Ruby, but of course, you thought you could! Some horses are fine at home in the environments they're used to but go wild with fear in new surroundings and routines.

"Start taking more thought to your own safety. You have people who love and need you. I love you, Ruby, but we'll explore that later.

"Until then get it into your beautiful, stubborn head that you're not a one-girl-show! Your uncle will have somethin' to say about this. He and I can't stand the thought of you being hurt. Think about Bowie next time. What would he do without you? He's been devastated since you got hurt."

Mostly from the frustration of feeling physically weak but also for the reprimand she'd just gotten, a tear rolled down her cheek and Ruby's bottom lip pushed out in a pout. Marcus had made quite a speech and she supposed she deserved it. Now she was tired and could hardly keep her eyes open. The effects of the laudanum were playing with her emotions and energy again. Her lip trembled.

Marcus's reserve was drained, and he leaned in to kiss her–a long, deep kiss–deepening even more to deliver a message. He softened the kiss and sucked tenderly. He lingered on that sweet bottom lip that he'd wanted to taste for so long. Ruby feigned to push him away, but she didn't try very hard. He took advantage of the opportunity and kissed Ruby one more time using his tongue to entice her lips to part. After a moment, he disengaged very gently and studied her carefully to measure the affect.

"Oh, Ruby. You can never again say that you haven't been kissed again. I am honored to be your first," he smiled. "It's entirely your fault, you know. What did I tell you about sticking that bottom lip out?" he asked teasingly as he outlined it with his index finger. "You tempted me one too many times, darlin', and see what it got you? Can't say I didn't warn you, Sunshine Girl. Don't ever torment me and expect to get away with it too often. You'd best remember that."

As she was drifting away, Ruby whispered one more time that she intended to return to the herd. Marcus could barely make out her words, "This place reminds me too much of—anyway, I don't--not here--"

As he kissed her cheek soundly, he could barely make out her words. "I'll be back in a few days, sweetheart. You rest and heal some. You'll be able to ride by then or you can ride double with me. Little Flower will see to you and I promise I'll come back.

"You'll be safe here, Ruby. I can guarantee it." Later these very words would come back to haunt Marcus.

As soon as Bowie and Hart, Little Flower's son, came in from doing chores, Marcus and Bowie rode out. All the way back to the herd, Marcus's mind was on Ruby Red.

*Damn! My woman is strong, smart, sassy and capable.*

*Thank you, God. You led me right to her and made it so I couldn't get away!*

He was concerned by her being upset to sit tight where she was for a few days. She had to know that his word was good. It was the laudanum clouding her judgment. When her fuzzy head cleared, she'd realize he'd be back for her.

As expected, Pete had kept moving the herd farther away but a blind man could track them. Pete had taken them to the next water and then laid over to wait for Marcus, Ruby and Bowie to catch up. The cattle and horses could rest and use the good grass available to maintain their strength and weight.

Jess was visibly relieved to hear Marcus say that Ruby

was on the mend. The stress of waiting to hear word was lined on his leathery face. All the boys whooped and hollered on finding out that Ruby would be back with them in a few days.

When camp settled down for the night, he cornered Jess.

"Okay, Marcus, what's on your mind? Somethin's eatin' at ya. I could see a dark cloud hanging over your head when you rode in today."

"Jess, John Blake asked me specifically to look after Ruby and Bowie. I messed up! I should've been watching her more closely. I should have been working where she was working. What possessed her to take that spooked horse off without tellin' nobody? Why did she think she could ride him out when no one else could?"

"Well–that's how Ruby thinks. I've been trying to look after her for a long time and it takes more than one to do the job. I've seen her make a lot of dicey moves and more often than not she can handle it. I've witnessed John going head-to-head with her on a number of unwise choices she's made. I've never known of him to be able to keep her from harm every time either. You'd have to tie that girl up every day as soon as she crawls out of bed to keep her from doing as she pleases. You'd have to break her spirit and that would be an out-and-out shame. The results wouldn't be worth it. Marcus, you can't beat yourself up over this.

"Maybe you'll be the one who can rein her in and tame her some. It'll be a task, I'm tellin' ya."

"I don't know, Jess–I just don't know.

"There's another thing. I hated leavin' her today. She was troubled about me leavin' her. I had to. She couldn't even raise herself off the bed without gasping. She said that it looked a lot like the place she and Bowie lived in before. I reassured her that I'd come back in a couple of days. I wouldn't have ridden off if I wasn't sure she had taken a turn for the better and was in a safe place. I still think it was the right thing to do but it's made me feel uneasy. She didn't want to stay."

"You did the best you could. You did right so quit second-guessing yourself. No good could come from having her bounce and jar on a horse to come back here when she's comfortable and healing in a decent place. You did exactly what I would have done.

"You'll come to understand Ruby more by and by. She acts strong as nails and she is but there's a part of her that's still an unhappy, terrified, nine-year-old who got abandoned when her folks were killed. She struggles with that.

"I think learning to care about you is a good thing. You're givin' her a reason to hope. She'll find out she doesn't have to be alone anymore. She'll always deal with the past but she's gonna' see she can put it down sometimes too. Believe me! It's hard for her to trust. Trust can turn into love, Marcus."

## CHAPTER 33

From a ridge hidden well by rocks and scrubs a hard-faced vaquero from Trank James's rag-tag group of cockroaches watched the woman's violent spill as it played out. From the distance he could hear the horse scream and later the shots that were fired. After that only the horse could be heard struggling. He could not tell if the fall had killed the girl until her friends came. They tried to revive the woman.

She was put on a travois and taken away by two people. From the direction they headed out, it was evident that she was being taken to the source of the smoke in the distance. Staying out of sight, the Mexican trailed the two cowboys pulling the travois with the girl.

Now, in a cold camp he was waiting a safe distance from the cabin. He ate cold beans wrapped in tortillas. The Mexican buzzard watched as the men rode out the next day without the woman. It was then he flew back to the base camp to report what he'd been circling.

Trank had been moving his band periodically to follow the herd. He'd been sending scouts out daily to keep eyes on the herd and the woman he sought to abduct. The woman was a play-pretty for his disgusting, filthy little brother. He almost felt sorry for her. Jake was weakened with a sickness in his gut and a mangled jaw from a beating he'd taken. He reeked disgustingly like a hot outhouse.

Trank had no idea what his little brother wanted or thought he could do with the girl once he had her nor did he really care. He'd never been fond of Jake before his childhood accident and certainly not after it either. He loathed looking after him when they were kids. He'd always been weak and more trouble than he was worth. Trank had taken several severe lickings that he'd never forget because of the little bastard!

For years now, he'd kept him quiet and away from him by making sure he had plenty of spending money. Why he now felt the burning need of a female companion was beyond Trank. His little brother's balls had been crushed in a farm accident when he was little. An old horse doctor had castrated the mangled flesh. He'd been left with a forever-wilted and useless member.

The accident had been entirely Trank's fault and he admitted to it. For that reason, he felt like he owed him something even though he detested him. In Trank's twisted mind it was Jake's doing that his drunken pa beat him unmercifully over the years. He'd finally slit the old bastard's throat while he was sleeping and left home.

His pa administered the first beating right after the accident. He'd nearly beaten him to death and Trank could almost justify that one. He was guilty of causing his brother's de-manning but there was no excuse for continuing the beatings.

To Jake's credit, he'd never asked Trank for much of anything. He sent him money willingly to compensate for being maimed and to keep him out of his hair. Trank was shocked recently when Jake asked him for a specific woman. It was a ludicrous idea, but Trank intended to see that he had her for a while at least. Afterwards, he could finally consider his debt paid in full. He'd put the obligation to an end once and for all.

Jake had always been twisted and perverted in how he thought. He was evil like Trank but in a demented, nasty way. The sniveling weasel suffered a pounding at his last job that left his body not only weak but failing him too.

This woman was connected to the man who had done this to him so Trank figured Jake was out for revenge. Jake had talked about killing the cowboy too. Trank had no qualms about killing so it made no difference to him if that's what his brother wanted.

His only interest in this was nabbing the girl and trading her back for the Triple B herd. He'd do it nice and easy like. He'd tie the guy up so Jake could be the one to murder him. The heady violence would offer a certain amount of entertainment. Then he planned to turn on Jake and kill him. It would be a mercy-killing the way he saw it. He'd put his brother out of his hellish misery on earth. Trank would never have to think of him again. It would be a win for both of them. Jake could die and Trank would be free of him.

The grubby vaquero rode into the outlaws' camp. After Trank listened to the whole report, he grinned broadly.

"Well, well! She's just a sitting duck waiting to be plucked from the pond. I couldn't have planned this set-up more neatly than if I'd figured it out myself. Take two men with you and get her. When you get back here, throw her in with Jake and guard her.

"While you're gone, we'll nab her kid brother and rough him up to make our point—show them what our work looks like–give them something to think about. The boy can deliver a note for us. We'll send a message loud and clear to the trail boss and her lover that we have the girl and mean business. We won't quite kill the kid, but he'll wish he was dead! One look, and they'll be begging to trade their herd for the pretty gal."

"What of that Indian lover and his squaw?" The vaquero sneered as he wiped rivers of bean juice from his creased chin using a flap of tortilla. He disgustingly wadded it into his mouth.

"Do what you want–have your sport–kill them–it's not important to me! Do whatever amuses you. Just bring the girl back alive and untouched. Don't leave marks on her! Save that privilege for my brother."

"Si!"

The ruthless outlaws rode out long before dawn leading an extra mount.

Jake James waited in the dank, dark, moldy tent that reeked of his peculiar foulness. The ever-present bandana tied to support his sagging jaw was soiled. He rarely came out into the air except at night when the camp was sleeping. He'd given up trying to clean himself and made little effort anymore. It was a losing battle and he felt too miserable and compromised to care any longer.

The awful smell of death and decay was not one that could be washed away. Something was festering inside his body. Food and fresh water were set outside his tent every day, but the food was not compatible with his injuries. What little he ate only made his suffering worse.

No one came to check on him or talk to him. His stench and his sagging face were intolerable to smell and look upon. He had become a grotesque monster. Jake was a walking dead man emaciated down to skin and bones. He'd not been able to chew or keep water down for days. Mostly he slept and was in and out of lucidness.

Earlier in the day from up wind, Trank told him Ruby

was near and would be brought soon. Even in his lowly physical state Jake looked forward to finally having his obsession next to him. Perhaps she could fix things.

# CHAPTER 34

The three heartless vaqueros rode brashly into the settlers' clearing making a racket like coyotes. Ruby heard the yips and throaty yelps and cursed Dobbs for abandoning her. She'd heard those bone-chilling sounds before and dreaded what would come next. The farmer rushed out of the door with a shotgun to protect his family. He was ready to fire but was gunned down before he could get one shot off.

The assassins stepped over his body to cross the threshold. A weakened Ruby had her gun in hand, but it was kicked away and thudded against the wall. Knocking her down with a hard fist one of the men drug her out in the sun by her hair. She scrabbled with her booted feet to keep up and try to regain footing, but it was useless.

Behind her Little Flower was yanked screaming out the door. She screamed louder and sobbed at the sight of her husband. He was lying lifelessly just beyond the door with his eyes and mouth wide open. Her shock and grief sounded like that of a wounded animal.

Hart, who'd come out of the barn at the sound of the commotion, was quickly roped under his armpits and dragged behind a horse back and forth in the yard. The outlaws tired of the game as soon as his cries and struggling stopped. The two women's heads were held roughly so they could not turn away from the atrocity. Nothing would ever erase the sweet boy's cries and pleas from Ruby's brain.

Ruby felt helpless with the loss of her gun. Her big hunting knife lay on the end of her bed and now she was held by her arms secured at her back with a piece of scratchy hemp. She had been rushed, outnumbered and up the creek before her foggy mind could process what was happening. Everything went down so fast that Ruby couldn't defend herself let alone anyone else. It became clear to her how the raiders had gotten the drop on her father and why he was unable to defend her precious mother and their home.

Ruby thought she'd prepared herself for surprise attacks. She'd thought herself ready and capable of defeating trash like these men. She'd thought herself ready for any danger. Just now did she realize the impossibility of one woman taking down bandits alone. They had the advantage. She slumped in absolute defeat and ceased to resist.

One of the Mexicans scoffed at her weakness and backhanded her hard several times across the face. Another reminded the other two in Spanish that this woman was not to be touched. All three were disgruntled. They wanted a taste of the ripe, young, yellow-haired white woman. They admired her large tits. They pinched and tormented them. They slapped her backside repeatedly laughing at her barrage of protests spoken in Spanish. Thick, angry whelps had been raised on the cheeks of her face and other places hidden by her clothes.

Ruby understood most of the words spoken out of their foul mouths and she certainly knew what the rude and offensive hand gestures meant. She was still recovering from her previous injuries. Their cruel abuse made her ribs ache. It was useless to do anything but try and survive.

The bloodied boy was left for dead where he lay. The men stripped and violated Little Flower and forced Ruby to watch and listen to her begging for them to stop. Each took his turn under her skirts and then took another. She no longer saw this woman but saw her mother instead. It was her mother's cries of suffering all over again!

The raping of Little Flower was obscene. The last man twisted the good woman's neck until it snapped like a stick. Her head lolled to the side at an unnatural angle. The sound of it was one more detail Ruby could never erase. Leaving her ravished body lying exposed in the dirt they all laughed and slapped their thighs like this had been nothing more than a clever party trick.

By this time, Ruby's thoughts were cycling between present atrocities and past atrocities. She knew a similar fate awaited her that had befallen her mother. Chaos and noise were flashing through her head from the past. Chaos and noise were surrounding her in the present.

*Praise God–Marcus–you got Bowie to safety–thank you, Marcus.*

With that last clear thought freeing her from responsibility, she started drifting into a place far above what was happening. She withdrew away from conscious thinking. Without feeling any hope, she slipped into a state of shock. Her psyche was mercifully transported into a trance-like suspension. A fog seemed to separate her body and mind and kept them from working together. The now and the past melded into dream-like hallucinations. She stared straight ahead oblivious of the noises and ruin going on around her. Then mercifully the world grew dark and no longer existed to her at all.

She was in a tree where she'd known security.

*My tree!*

She was safe and comfortable with dry breezes brushing her cheeks and displacing wisps of hair around her face like soft feathers. Big River was grazing not far away. She had only to whistle and he would come to her. She knew Jess was standing below waiting to catch her like always.

In the far distance a rider approached. She shaded her eyes to bring the mirage into focus.

*Of course! It's my cowboy. All I must do is await him. He's coming for me. He promised.*

She concentrated as hard as she could to see all the wavering images blending together as one. She felt herself racing Big River at full speed toward the row of trees. Then he was gone too.

She climbed the tree over and over in her mind until she was exhausted.

*Why can't I reach the top?*

Ruby looked down for Jess to soothe her but saw Marcus instead. She was momentarily calmed by a promise, but she couldn't quite hear him what he was saying.

That's when she saw Ma and Pa! They were together holding hands and looking right as rain. Happiness glowed on their faces! They were encouraging her, but she couldn't make out the words.

She shrieked but she couldn't hear any sound. Maybe she didn't really scream, but the abrupt effort left her throat raw. Ruby drifted in and out of reality like this for what seemed like hours. One side was warm, familiar and soothing. The other side was hot, upsetting and torturous. She was fearful.

Suddenly, she experienced a rush of awareness as she barreled back to consciousness and landed on a broomtail. It took some time to realize her feet were bound together under the horse and her wrists were secured to a saddle horn. Her ribs were on fire and she was slumped over the animal and having difficulty breathing. She had no strength and her head was splitting.

The laudanum had worn off and the pain was unbearable. She had a powerful urge to relieve herself, but no one would listen to her.

*Stop! Why won't Marcus let me stop?*

Finally, her bladder emptied of its own free will. Hot urine ran in the saddle and dripped down her legs into her boots. Droplets plopped in the dust below leaving tiny craters. Soon her skin would be scalded and blistered raw between her legs and on her bottom.

Her mouth was dried out as if it was filled with powder. Ruby was powerfully thirsty and need for water consumed her, but she had none. Her tongue was thickened, and she could hardly swallow. Her lips were dried, cracked and bleeding.

*What kind of hell is this?*

Ruby became alert with a start only to be assaulted by the most fetid of smells. They pervaded her nostrils and choked her. She fought to identify the source of the stench. She cried out when she realized she was sitting in her own body wastes, but she could not be the cause of all the odors. There was just too much and she was overwhelmed!

*Shit–shit and lots of it–vomit–urine–sweat–wait, calm down and think–where am I?*

That's when she became aware of a loose, oily smelling bag covering her head and tied around her neck. Ruby started taking a mental inventory of things she knew for sure.

She was no longer moving but flat on her back. Her arms and hands were tied, and her boots were bound together. She wanted to leave but she was hobbled like a horse. Every inch of her body ached. She'd never been in a place quite like this before. The smell was the inside of a rotting carcass if she had to guess. She was gagging from the putrid air and her head tossed from side to side trying to dislodge the hot sack. The skin burned where the abrasive rope had rubbed her wrists raw. She could see nothing. Hot tears rolled down her face and she knew she was securely trapped.

*Why?*

She could hear sounds of occupation coming from a distance along with muffled voices. Ruby jumped when close by a weak, creaky, gravelly voice croaked just above a whisper.

"Ruby–mmmyRuby–you'reawakekeke–I've      been waiting–for so longngngng–my on pr–tty girl–"

The feeble voice creaked like the devil himself taunted her.

"You're–okayay–Rub–no one hurt you againnnn–you're backckck–you belonggggg–I hav you now–all–put right. I--not let you–go–"

The devil broke into a coughing fit. He coughed up more vile smells, spitting disgustingly. Then all went quiet except for labored breathing. Ruby couldn't place the congested voice, but it had called her by name.

*Who is that? Lord, this is a nightmare! Where am I? Please send Marcus for me.*

She was so disoriented that she couldn't discern up from down. The bafflement of not knowing when, where and what plus the physical pain attacking her body was debilitating. The fear and helplessness of the situation wrecked her mind. If she didn't believe Marcus was truly on his way, she might die of despair.

*Hurry, Marcus–I'll do whatever it takes to survive–I want to be here when you come–hurry, please!*

From close by she heard the coughing, wheezing and muttering again. Her senses overloaded with sour smells and she gagged spewing her own bitter, scorching bile. She was disgusting. She still needed water. She would surely die of dehydration.

*God, please just strike me dead. Make it a quick death. It will be a relief. Send Marcus, please. I'm realizing things and if I get out of here, I'm going to change. Get me back to my people.*

Exhaustion and despair flooded her mind with random wishes. Some fit together and some didn't. She was all mixed up and beyond miserable. She was disoriented with no reference point between day and night. She had no way to measure time.

She slipped in and out of restless sleep filled with disconnected dreams.

# CHAPTER 35

Marcus left the herd long before day break. He was anxious and frantic to get back to Ruby. He led Big River for her but if Ruby didn't feel up to riding, she could sit on Bob and he would cradle her. They could travel slowly on the way back. He was hopeful that she would be well enough to sit on her horse but the thought of holding her close was not unpleasant.

He'd had an uneasy feeling since leaving her behind that something wasn't right. Maybe he should have stayed with her but he couldn't send Bowie and Whiskey back to the herd by themselves. No! He'd made the only decision he could considering all circumstances. He was sure that Ruby was seeing it that way by now too. The last couple of days had given the rest needed for her to start healing and make it easier to ride back tomorrow.

It had allowed him a lot of time to think as well. He decided he would persuade Ruby to marry him as soon as they reached Abilene. John Blake would be happy to see them harnessed. He'd already made that abundantly clear. Marcus feared that she was not ready for what marriage entailed but he was willing to move slowly on that front.

They would cross that bridge together. Being married would give him the right to shamefully tease, touch and tutor her in how good he could make her feel.

When he got close to the homestead the horses tensed with the scent of spilled blood, backing up and snorting. It was so strong that he could smell it too and his stomach recoiled. He'd seen the buzzards circling from a distance and feared immediately that things were wrong. He drew his gun without thinking. It was only a moment before he saw the homesteader and Little Flower lying in front of the cabin. A short distance away lay Hart's body.

"Where's Ruby—where is she?" Marcus asked this out loud but Big River only tossed his head and sidestepped. "We've got to find her!" Desperation sounded in his voice.

His mind raced as his eyes darted here, there and back again in search of a fourth body, but he didn't see it. He cautiously dismounted with his gun at the ready. Carefully stepping over the settlers, he cautiously entered the house by the open door. He called out her name. The only sign of Ruby was her hat without the turquoise band. The bandana she'd tied around her hair on the day of the accident was thrown across the room. The cabin had been ransacked. His heart sank but he knew that not finding a body meant she could still be alive. Whoever did this must have taken her with them.

First, he had to bury these good, innocent people who were hurt trying to help them. He could not leave them lying there so that he could leave to find her. The family had sacrificed too much already. They couldn't be left lying in the sun for animals to feast upon. He'd turn their animals loose to fend for themselves before he left. They'd die of starvation if left in the pens. He gathered the gruesome bodies of the man and woman. He straightened them side by side and covered them with a thick Indian blanket from the house. They deserved to be handled with respect. He planned to dig one big grave for all three bodies.

Kneeling by the boy to collect his body the sound of a barely audible moan startled him. He wasn't dead yet but not far from it! Part of the rope used to drag him was still looped around his body.

Marcus did everything within his power to help Hart Preston. He was a gentle, good-looking kid who was only a few years younger than Bowie. Bowie and Whiskey had accepted him as a friend right away. The boy remained unconscious but had rallied just long enough to take a few swallows of water. He was not lucid or able to shed information about Ruby or the men who had done this. Though his skin was scraped away from many areas of his body, his face had not taken the brunt of the trauma. It was pure luck that he'd been able to keep his head up enough to minimalize damage to his face.

Marcus cleaned and bandaged him as best he could by using water and whiskey to stave off infection. The ministrations were mercifully enough to cause the boy to pass out again each time he rallied. He applied Little Flower's medicinal salve that he'd found thrown to the floor in the cabin.

Marcus had hoped to bury the family quickly and go after Ruby. Finding Hart alive changed his plans. He hooked the travois used for transporting her a few days ago to Bob and carefully loaded Hart onto it.

A sob escaped from his throat as he tied Ruby's hat onto Big River's saddle. Marcus took out for the herd with Hart in tow. It was a long ride and he stopped often to check on Hart and offer him water. With the two good horses he rode steadily all night. At first, he had to coax Big River to accept him as a rider or to pull the load. After soothing him, the smart stallion seemed to understand this was an important job. Ruby's horse wanted his mistress as much as Marcus needed his lady.

The camp was all in a dither when Marcus rode in with

Hart and no Ruby. Marcus was depending on Pete and Jess to help him get her back. Jess could cover doctoring Hart better than he could. The tough, young boy was holding his ground and had born the travel well. Marcus prayed that he'd make it with no infection.

Marcus's heart was wrenched tighter as he was led to Bowie lying beneath the cook wagon. He'd been beaten within an inch of his life. His face was so swollen that he could hardly be recognized. Marcus held his hand and talked to him quietly trying to make sense of this. Whiskey lay by him bandaged around the middle and only raised his head slightly in recognition.

The trail drive that had started out as a splendid adventure had now turned into a full-fledged, nightmarish string of events. Marcus had not been able to keep either Ruby or Bowie safe as he had promised John. Things had gotten complicated and out of hand quickly.

He grimaced listening to Pete telling how Bowie and Whiskey had disappeared from night watch and hadn't been found until the next morning. He had a broken arm and a couple of busted ribs. His face was swollen but no facial bones had been broken. All his teeth were intact. Whiskey had been shot and left for dead, but the bullet had passed through without hitting anything vital. He was most likely trying to defend Bowie with his own body. Jess had done his best for both boy and the loyal dog.

A bloodied note had been pinned to Bowie's shirt demanding a trade for Ruby in exchange for the herd. It said that tomorrow at dusk, Ruby would be beaten. The whippings would continue nightly until arrangements for the trade were made to Trank James's satisfaction.

The cowboys were fidgeting in limbo waiting for Pete to tell them what to do. There would be no more driving the herd toward Abilene until they could figure out how to rescue Ruby from these spawns of the devil. At least they knew she was alive, for now, but she was far from safe.

Marcus slipped out of sight away from the camp. He braced his body against a tree and didn't even try to hold back his tears of anguish in the cover of the brush. He stayed clear of the camp until he could regain his composure and get himself collected enough to make her rescue. His mind was in torment with concern over Ruby's condition after he'd seen what had been done to Bowie.

*Those vipers better not have violated you, darlin'? Are you hungry? Are you hurtin'? I'm coming!*

His thoughts were crushing his spirit. He had to get his wits together or he wouldn't be sane enough to be useful to her. Waiting around ate at him but there had to be a plan. He didn't even know which way to go.

Jess now had both Bowie, Whiskey and Hart under the cook wagon. He had his hands full tending them. He was pleased to see that there was no sign of infection on the younger boy. Marcus had given him good care when he found him. The boy had cried as Jess rewashed his wounds with whiskey and checked for any sign of festering or fever. One of the cowboys held the boy down while Jess tended him. It was a grim task but had to be done regardless of the pain. He reapplied the same salve Marcus had found at the homestead. Now the boy was resting naked under a light cover to allow air to get to his scrapes. They needed to dry. Both boys were given laudanum to ease their pains and allow them the blessing of a deep sleep. Mostly they would require care and time for healing. Jess would get them to a doctor in Abilene as soon as possible.

As tired as Marcus was, he stayed up to calculate the next move with Pete and Jess. Pete had sent out scouts to find and get a bead on the layout of the thieves' camp. They were not able to pinpoint exactly where Ruby was being held but there was a tent where they assumed she might be. They had seen food being delivered there. They also counted fifteen rough-looking men armed to the teeth.

# CHAPTER 36

Just after day break eight men rode from the direction of Abilene into the trail camp. One was John Blake! He shed indiscrete tears over finding Bowie, the young boy and Whiskey. They were the victims of horrendous crimes. When he heard about Ruby's plight he was visibly shaken to the core. Marcus could hardly look Blake in the eye. John would have none of that. He embraced him like a son and they both swore to work together to get her back in one piece.

The boss had made it to Abilene and already arranged for the sale of the cattle. The contract was waiting for the number of head to actually be delivered. When he'd finally discovered who had sabotaged the stock car orders, John knew by the information that it had to be Jake and Trank James behind it. He went immediately to the Texas Rangers' office for help to get the herd into Abilene safely.

Trank James, was a dangerous man at the very top of the Rangers' most wanted list. They had been most interested in what Blake had to say. They'd been trying to stop his killing and looting for a while. The killer was illusive. They followed any lead that might lead to his apprehension.

Putting two and two together, it was easy for them to agree that Trank was after the herd with his brother acting as an accomplice.

Three rangers and four other lawmen accompanied John to meet up with his outfit. They were counting on finally putting Trank and his gang out of circulation. This was the best lead they'd had to date, and nothing was going to stand in their way. It came as a shock that Bowie had been hurt badly and Ruby was being held hostage. The story of Mr. and Mrs. Preston's murders and Hart being dragged and left for dead made their blood run cold. They solemnly listened to the tragic accounts.

After listening to reports from the scouts Pete had sent out, a strategic plan was formulated. The Ranger Captain took charge of the operation. Everyone had to follow his orders or not participate in any way. With the authority of the Texas rangers and the additional help from the extra lawmen, they'd storm Trank's camp. Hopefully, Ruby could be rescued alive and the notorious outlaw could be captured at the same time.

The command was given that they would move in at dusk. Tension mounted heavily since the note stated Ruby would be beaten around that time. The Captain felt that dusk would provide the best cover and that Ruby was likely to be brought out into the open then. Trank enjoyed audiences to witness his violent acts of cruelty. John and Marcus were grim at the risk this placed on Ruby.

Ruby fought to take her mind back to the tree but that didn't work anymore. The pain and uncertainty of her situation kept breaking her concentration. The man who occupied the tent with her continually mumbled and feebly groped her body. She could not recollect who he was but was certain that he must know her. She had yet to see his face because of the sack cutting off her vision. His smell had caused her to dry heave until her throat was sore and swollen. She could not stomach the frijoles brought to her or keep the dirty water down. She was severely thirsty. Her head was still covered but the scratchy bag had been loosened at the neck so a cup and food could be held to her mouth. Several times she had been pulled from the tent to relieve her body only to be humiliated with more groping and laughter from dirty men speaking a Spanish dialect common to Texas.

Thankfully, she'd been allowed to keep her boots on her feet. At the first opportune time she would try to use the knife hidden in the lining of one of them. She would have to wait until she was freed of the sack so she could see. There was no doubt that given the chance she would stick to kill. Wounding was not an option! She couldn't fight all the men, but she planned to kill at least one of them.

Ruby sensed things were about to change when she was man-handled roughly and dragged to the middle of the camp. She was untied and the bag removed. She was made to sit on a large rock. She had a hard time focusing her eyes. She'd been denied light for so long and she was sick.

She was stunned to look into the faces of the hard, dispassionate outlaws who were clearly hungry for entertainment. It wasn't hard to figure out that she would be the dancer at this party. She felt like a piece of meat being thrown into the lion's den. She was sure that whatever was about to happen would take place very soon. The tension of expectation was rising around her as the noise level increased.

Surveying her surroundings, she took in every detail. She was surrounded by pitiless men. If she tried to run, they would stop her. Straight out escaping was not an option. With her hands now free she could seriously consider using the sharp-bladed knife concealed in her boot. It was the only chance she had, and she could not afford to waste it. Timing was everything.

Unknown to Ruby the Rangers had positioned men in place and were observing the scene below. They would not make a move to save her unless the exact and right situation presented itself. Putting this gang of thugs out of commission was more important to the government than the life of one girl.

When she had been dragged to the center of the camp Marcus cringed at the site of her condition. She was pale, filthy, bruised and weakened. The over-abundance of self-assurance and sass that was Ruby was gone. His darlin' cowgirl was in trouble.

He had the strong urge to go to her regardless of the outcome. The Captain threatened to order him back if he couldn't stand down. It took all of the will power he could muster but he managed to stay still and quiet. He had no intention of leaving her to fend for herself ever again.

Trank James, the bear-like man who was the leader, appeared as dusk was engulfing the camp. The dancing flames of the bonfire cast eerie, evil silhouettes across the scene. He was grasping a stout leather strap with his fat sausage-like fingers. One end was wrapped around the palm of his hand. A thick cigar was balanced in the corner of his surly mouth. His fake laugh was loud and sounded like the devil. His minions cheered a welcome raring to go.

He was almost salivating as he expertly snapped the air with the strap causing his men to nod their heads, laugh hungrily and shout uncouth encouragements. It was obvious this was not the first demonstration of the strap they'd attended. Like dogs with a taste for blood they waited eagerly salivating while looking forward to the spectacle. The orange fire illuminated their faces making them fiendish in appearance.

The backs of Ruby's shirt and camisole were suddenly rent from top to bottom. The knife carelessly sliced her sweet skin between her shoulder blades allowing a beading of blood to slip down and puddle at the small of her back. The crowd roared with approval demanding more.

Roughly jerking the cut edges of fabric apart to expose her entire bare back, the two henchmen pushed her face down on the rock. They held her arms out to the side and spread her legs by kicking her feet apart. They clamped them in place with pressure from their boots. One of them gathered and grabbed her long hair and jerked it to the side so hard that the action pulled her head back before her face was slammed back to the rock.

To keep from calling a halt to Ruby's inescapable lashing Marcus clenched his tongue between his teeth until he could taste his own blood. The grizzly outlaw began strapping her back with a force that broke the skin leaving behind bloody tracks. Her body shuddered and lifted like a puppet with each stinging blow. Marcus could not watch, nor could he look away.

*God, put an end to this. Let me take the whipping in her stead. Please, God.*

He prayed and begged for this misery to come to an end. He willed his mind to share his strength with Ruby. Each crack made his body jerk with hers as if he was the one being hit.

She tried her hardest not to scream as she repeatedly tried to free herself from the men who held her down. She kept her silence for what seemed like forever, but the agony and anguish became too much. Her resolve broke like a dam and she emitted piteous cries and sobs. She had no way of knowing that Marcus was with her and tears of pain were running down his face freely.

Unexpectedly, the decimated skeleton-like body of Jake James emerged from the tent and he raised his arm weakly. He shot a small caliber handgun into the air. All eyes turned toward him.

He hoarsely croaked and yelled as best he could, "Stoppp–leave be–longs to meeee–Ruby–let her goooo..."

Trank paused disgustedly and turned. All eyes were on Jake. Trank James drew his gun, aimed and shot his own brother a death blow to the chest. Not even waiting for his sibling to hit the ground he turned around to raise the strap to Ruby's lacerated back again. In that same instance pandemonium had broken out in the camp from every direction spurred by the command shouted by the Texas Ranger Captain. Confusion registered on the faces of the outlaws. Ruby's captors released the iron grip they had been securing her with and fled for their own lives.

A surge of adrenaline ignited Ruby's muscles empowering them with a flash of strength. She took advantage in that split second of chaos to pull the knife from her boot. In a fluid motion, she turned as she was simultaneously pulling out the knife and threw swiftly with a deadly accuracy that penetrated Trank's black heart. He seemed momentarily suspended in the air. His mouth formed an O-shape as if it dawned on him for one brief second what was happening. His knees buckled and he fell backwards like David's Goliath. His big, ugly head landed in the fire of hell and the flames demanded hot justice for his soul!

Marcus, with gun drawn, was making his way pell-mell to Ruby under the cover of the bedlam reigning. He didn't know that she'd thrown her knife killing the monster. He didn't even know that she had a knife. He had begun running the gauntlet of bullets as soon as the Rangers, lawmen and cowboys rose to advance. The only thing he was sure of was that Ruby had gone down to the ground in front of the rock. He panicked fearing the worst.

He was a raging bull charging toward the love of his life firing shots at shadows as he ran toward her. Nothing was going to keep him from the woman he loved any longer. With the sounds of a gunfight still raging from every direction he reached his target. His strong, decisive arms folded around her trembling body protectively. The shaking was blessed evidence that she was alive. Men continued to yell, fall and run all around in every direction. He moved her behind the protection of the rock covering her broken body with his own.

Not understanding who had hold of her now or that she was safe, she fought with a strength fed again by a fresh burst of adrenalin. Her arms were stilled to submission as a man's body covered hers like a shield of protection. She no longer felt threatened. She faintly began to hear her name and sweet words like sunshine soothing her over and over again. The words sounded distant, hollow and blunt as if coming from the bottom of a deep well. She heard them in slow motion.

Sweet gratitude flooded her heart. She knew this voice

*He came for me–Marcus came---he came--thank you, God, thank you!*

She felt an immediate, profound peace. It was Marcus and she ceased to be afraid. The surges of energy she'd had were drained and spent. She lay against him like a wet noodle. Her body collapsed as if it was boneless. He softly kissed every square inch of her bruised face. He covered it in a sugary wetness. He was oblivious to her soured and foul odor as his love for her covered it all. Smells were insignificant compared to his relief in finding Ruby alive. The thunderous chaotic din around them gradually calmed to the muted sounds of organized, benign recovery.

# CHAPTER 37

A canteen of cool water was held to her lips and she drank greedily but choked, spitting it back up. She thought she heard Uncle John's voice but could not make out the words. Her eyelids were so heavy that though she tried to open them the effort failed. There were other men's voices all around discussing things insistently. The drone of the words irritated her.

She pressed into Marcus's embrace tightly with her face buried in his hard chest. She was engulfed in the throbbing pain that was her body and the confusion that was her mind. She clung to him like a leach seeking to latch on for his life blood. She would not be separated from him ever again. Never again! This one thing she desired more than anything.

*I need your strength–Marcus.*

Her body started shaking uncontrollably from shock and she heard herself crying like a little girl. Once started, the tears were endless. Marcus's chest rumbled with something he was saying but she could only feel the vibrations of his words but did not hear them. All the voices around her were indistinguishable, hollow and faceless. Even the familiarity of Uncle John's voice had collapsed along with the many gruff voices falling away like autumn leaves. Either she could not move, hear or see or her mind chose not to bother with those actions. Her mind was frozen, numb and encapsulated in shock.

Marcus stroked her dirty, sticky hair while whispering sweet, loving things to her. She sensed the meanings of the words not from understanding but from the inflections. He allowed her to stay undisturbed in his arms trying to be careful of her ripped and bleeding back. Maybe she slept but she didn't know because she felt oddly detached. She'd shifted away from awareness of activity around her.

Marcus carried her all the way to the stream. He gently removed her ruined clothing and carefully took her into the water. Supporting her he washed her body lovingly with the soap Jess had handed him. He washed her hair, her face, her arms and her sweet breasts. She whimpered out as he leaned her forward over one arm and gently scrubbed the raw open stripes crisscrossing her back. The ministrations left them fresh and bleeding again. He hated this but it needed to be done. An infection could kill her. He choked and sobbed on the words as he apologized and sympathized over and over for hurting her.

In the shadows of the moonlight and under the cover of the water he gently and respectfully washed between her legs and buttocks where blistering caused by prolonged exposure to body wastes flared angrily. Going and coming, in and out of lucidness, she was beyond feeling humiliation or shame. She trusted this man. Ruby relinquished her care to him completely and clung to him like a child. She accepted his presence as a comfort.

She had known in her heart he would come for her. She never doubted it. She was not concerned about what

Marcus was doing to her. She was too exhausted to do for herself. Finished, he carried her to a soft pallet spread out by John and turned her lightly onto her stomach covering her to the waist after medicating her from the bottle of laudanum Jess handed him. He coaxed her into swallowing the bittersweet-tasting liquid and promised it would ease her pain. She fell into a restless sleep.

After settling Ruby, it was Jess's turn to doctor her. Washing her injuries had left Marcus unsteady and he took his own much needed bath and reprieve. He scrubbed vigorously in the stream while Jess applied whiskey to Ruby's wounds. The old man put in practiced stitches and applied a soothing cream to her shredded back which he left exposed to the air.

All the while John held her steady and hovered stroking her head and talking very quietly to her as if she was still his little girl. Sometimes the sharp punctures caused her to cry out as the deepest of her lacerations were being pulled together. Soothing words delivered by both men offered comfort. She heard their caressing voices. Uncle John's voice mingled with Jess's words full of sympathy and concern. She slept more deeply now from the laudanum and pure exhaustion but also from feeling how loved she was by all three men.

John and Jess had a warm fire burning and a pan of stew simmered and steamed on the edge of it. The coffee was fresh and there were biscuits. Marcus pulled on clean clothes from his saddle bags as he heard the men talking softly. He joined them at the fire for hot coffee laced with whiskey. John passed out smokes.

All three faces mirrored the strain of the last couple of days and especially the last agonizing hours. There was joy and thanksgiving at finally having Ruby secured and tended under the umbrella of their safeguard. They knew more was injured than just the physical, but they'd help her with the rest later.

John handed Marcus a leather pouch. In it he found Ruby's guns, hunting knife, the boot knife used to kill Trank and the turquoise headband. The guns had been taken off a dead vaquero and returned to John Blake. Marcus was confused to find a second headband similar to the other one.

He looked at John questioningly. "I don't understand."

"Apparently, one of the older gang members was involved in the raid on my brother's horse ranch or got this from someone who was. My brother and my sister-in-law had matching turquoise and silver hat bands. Ruby had the one belonging to her ma on the day, so many years ago, that she and Bowie were separated from their parents forever. I assumed the other had been lost in the fire. As you can see, I was wrong. Maybe having the second one back will bring some kind of closure for her and Bowie. They will finally feel that there is at least a symbolic retribution for their parents' deaths."

"John–Jess –," Marcus cleared his throat. "I'm claiming Ruby for my wife if you approve. I vow to marry her as soon as a preacher can be fetched to this spot. She's not leaving this place for several days and I'm staying right here with her. I want to be the one to take care of her. I love her."

John spoke first. "What will Ruby say to this notion of yours? I'm all for the two of you marrying–have been since you cornered her at the corral that day, but I can't speak for what Ruby will accept."

"She loves him, John, sure 'nuff," Jess broke in. "I've known for a time now and could see her tryin' to fight it.

"As for me, Marcus, I'd like to see you take her on– she'll be worth every gray hair you'll earn from her. I love her like my own grandchild. If you hurt her you'll have to answer to me!"

"Well, it seems you've passed the muster with Jess. It wouldn't be right if I didn't wholeheartedly give my blessings too.

"As for tending to Ruby–there aren't women here to help her along–out of necessity, it has to be one of us three. Jess must see to our boys & Whiskey. In fact, he needs to get back now. Since you've given your word as a man to claim her as your own, I think it's pretty much settled that it'll be you. Sometimes things have to get done out of order regardless of what's proper.

"Pete's pulling the herd out in the morning to get them to my buyers in Abilene. Bowie and Hart need to get to a doctor with Jess and rest-up in a clean room at a hotel. I'll be coming back with a doctor for Ruby and a preacher to marry ya'll as soon as possible.

"It's up to you to make her see what's what on the subject of marriage. If she's in a mind to marry you, she won't care if it's done under a tree instead of in town. I'm sure she'd like it better. We'll have a reception party back home later."

# CHAPTER

## CHAPTER 38

R uby was feeling and moving a little better by the next morning. She was stiff, sore, hurting and had to lie on her stomach but her head was clear. She could keep nourishment down. It was a good thing because she was weak as a kitten and needed the strength that food could give her. She was exhausted all the way to the bone.

She bathed in the cool water again to ease the pain from the scalded skin the unsanitary conditions had caused. Marcus applied more of the healing cream and removed the stitches from her head that Little Flower had applied. He held off giving her a dose of laudanum until she was settled back on the pallet. He'd been waiting for this chance to speak with her.

"I know you've been figuring on never marrying but that just don't seem right for a beautiful girl like you. That cherry pie you made proved that you can cook well enough. You already have practical experience raising a child–look how well Bowie's turning out! Ruby, you'd make a fine wife and mother someday and that's the truth.

"I think having a partner to share life with could be a good thing if you find a like-minded cowboy you can tolerate."

"What are you getting to with all this talking? Who would want to partner up with me? A man might expect his wife to quit raising horses and ranching–I won't give either up! I've worked too hard for the right all these years–I can't have a man bossing me every time I turn around either. I will not live like that, Marcus. I won't. If there was someone wanting to have me–which there isn't–he'd have to take me the way I am or not at all."

"I can appreciate that, sunshine, and I think I know just the man for you."

"Who would that be?"

"He's a man who already loves you just exactly the way you are. He needs you with him for every day of the rest of his life. It's a cowboy who doesn't care you might beat him at ropin' sometimes, outshoot him occasionally or even climb a tree when you take a notion. This man wants to partner with you raisin' horses and running cattle.

"I'm that man, Ruby Red. I love you more than my own life–marry me, hon–make me a lucky cowboy! Will you marry me?"

"Yes–yes–I know I love you too, Marcus. When I was being held captive, I decided if I ever got out alive, I'd do things differently. Wasting time fretting about atrocities that happened a long time ago or worrying about what might happen tomorrow isn't who I care to be anymore. I want to be happy–right now! I'd be proud to be your partner, Marcus. With what you know and what I know, we'll raise the finest horses in Texas! We'll learn together how to raise little cowboys and little cowgirls just like us!"

Marcus leaned in and kissed her like a man who'd just found home. He couldn't get enough. She allowed his tongue to explore her mouth and she did a little exploration herself. A sound of distress reminded him of Ruby's pain, so he pulled back. She was ready to accept a dose of laudanum. A peaceful sleep overtook her this time.

The wedding under a tree by the stream suited Ruby perfectly. It took place after a doctor from Abilene examined and treated her. He declared the wounds to be healing satisfactorily but warned her to be patient while she recovered her full health and strength. He cautioned her to take time to process the unfortunate things she'd suffered. The doctor advised her to talk and share her sadness and fears, so they'd have no power over her.

After that the knot was tied rather unceremoniously so she could rest again. Uncle John had a ring for Marcus to put on the finger of his new bride. Jess was there and so were Bob and Big River grazing unaware nearby.

# CHAPTER 39

Uncle John surprised his family by escorting a lovely lady to join the special supper in celebration of the new couple. He'd ordered it to be laid out in a private hotel room reserved for such occasions. He was proud as punch to introduce Miss Laura Birch to those he cherished most in the world. He explained they'd met a few years ago and kept in touch during his trips to Abilene.

Ruby was beautiful in an ecru lace dress and a white hat adorned with her mother's turquoise band. Marcus was a fine-looking cowboy in black with a hat sporting the turquoise band that had belonged to her father but rightfully belonged to Bowie now. He surprised his bride with a bouquet of blue wildflowers tied with a white fluffy ribbon and gifted her with a string of beautiful turquoise nuggets to wear around her neck.

John Blake was a contented man to see his niece had found such a fine match. He knew Marcus would make the Triple B Brand and his family proud. He had no doubt his brother and sister-in-law were smiling down from heaven at this very moment.

After the ordeal, Ruby had not hesitated to marry

Marcus. This was their wedding supper with champagne for toasting. The meal was delicious with fried chicken, mashed potatoes, gravy, hot rolls and green beans. Uncle John had ordered a white wedding cake served with peaches, cream and a fruity spiked punch.

After the gathering they dwindled away one after the other. The time had come for the newlyweds to retire to the honeymoon suite. The door clicked shut behind them.

Marcus whispered into Ruby's ear and caressed her neck, "Get ready for bed."

He felt her tense slightly. Ruby was a virgin and naturally nervous. They had put off coupling while she recuperated but the time had come.

Marcus and Ruby had been sharing a bed since they married but enjoying snuggling close and becoming familiar with each other was all they'd shared. She had needed the time for her body to heal. The mere thought of consummating their marriage now made her body tingle in the most private places.

Ruby took her nightgown into the water closet to take care of ablutions and change. She stalled taking unnecessary time. Finally, Marcus knocked on the door and she had no choice but to open it and step out to her husband. He was standing there in only his drawers which she had not been expecting. He saw the look of apprehension when her eyes briefly took in the taut fabric covering his manhood. He put his hand lightly on her shoulder in understanding.

"Ruby, I won't hurt you. Don't be afraid of me. We'll go slowly.

"Come here."

He guided her to the settee and pulled her onto his lap. "Ruby, you are the most precious, beautiful part of my life. I want you badly, but I would never take you in a selfish way. You trust me, don't you?

"Believe me, baby–look at me–look at me now! You are

a passionate woman. Haven't we been having a good time so far? Very soon I'll show you that you want me as much as I want you. We'll find our way together. I will never do anything you don't want. You can ask me to stop and I always will.

"I do plan on doing this though."

He pulled her gently into his hard, muscled chest. With one hand on her waist and one hand splayed in her yellow hair he caressed and hugged her. His heartbeat was strong and beating a little faster than usual.

She reached out a hand resting it tentatively against the tight, brown curls on his chest. She'd first seen these curls on that shameless day on the Rio Grande.

"That's right, Ruby. Touch me. Being together will never be something just for me. We're partners, remember, we'll both share the enjoyment."

He hugged her to him, and they remained that way for a moment. Then he lifted her chin with one knuckle and slowly lowered his lips to meet hers. At first, he touched her so lightly that he could barely feel his mouth meet hers. Then he took her lips with a warm pressure growing into a really deep kiss. He ended it by teasing her bottom lip the way she liked.

"I wanted to kiss my bride. Are you okay so far, Ruby?"

She nodded her head.

"How about this? Can I do this, sunshine?" He pushed back her hair on one side and laid a whole row of little quick, moist kisses along her neck making the skin tingle just above her shoulder. All the while he stroked her collar bone lightly with his thumb. He stopped raising his head slowly to search her eyes.

"Doing well, Ruby?"

"Yes, Marcus."

"Good, girl! I'm gonna' kiss you again."

This time he encompassed her whole mouth and

caressed it thoroughly with his lips and tongue applying more pressure than before. He used the tip of his tongue to stroke her plump lips. When she opened her mouth to take a breath, he took it as an invitation to enter her mouth assertively. He used his tongue in and out repeatedly mimicking what was to come. She accepted this treatment without complaint and deepened the kiss sucking until they were sharing the very breath that sustained them. He ended the petting by thoroughly sucking and licking her bottom lip. Then he stood with an arm around her waist helping her up.

"Do you feel easier now, hon?"

"Much better," she sighed.

"Let's go to bed now. We've had a big day and it's not over yet."

She climbed up into the high bed and under the covers. Marcus admired the shapely swell of her bottom as she did. He reached out and palmed the globes of her peach.

He climbed in and held her close. She returned the hug.

"I want to hold you, touch you and kiss you, Ruby, but we're wearing way too many clothes. I desire to be inside you as close as we can get."

They stripped quickly.

"That's real fine, Ruby. I believe you'll enjoy being together.

"Tell me what feels good to you or if I hurt you."

He slid an arm under her neck and rested one hand on the dip of her waist. With a knee he wedged her thighs open as he held himself over her body. Her sweet hair was an aphrodisiac to his arousal. The fresh smell of lilacs made him harder. It drew him to touch her center. "Like this, baby?"

"Mmmm, yessss–like this!"

He'd reached the decisive passion point within this woman. The delicious desire was the one she'd come to crave.

"Ruby, you may find my entering you will be uncomfortable for just a moment. I promise it won't last for long. After that, I'll make you feel better than you've ever felt before. That's a promise."

Marcus guided the head of his erection to the entrance of her treasure. He entered very slowly but not deep and withdrawing to enter again. He repeated this motion several times before he deepened the strokes until he could feel the resistance of her maidenhead.

The next long stroke seated him to the hilt. Ruby gasped slightly as he tore through the gate of her virginity. He stilled entirely until she recovered from his invasion. The deep strokes following were more aggressive. He reached a hand between them and thumbed her button until she arched her back to seal any space between them and she squirmed.

The spasms of her wall caused him to spill over the edge to his release and he felt the need to push inward farther and complete the sacred act of mating. As he retreated, they were both panting as if they'd just run a race. Marcus fell on his back beside her.

"What did I tell you, Ruby? Don't love feel grand?"

# EPILOGUE

From his vantage point on the knoll overlooking the ranch houses and buildings, Marcus could see how far his life had come since he first stepped foot on the Triple B. Being surrounded by family and friends gave him reason to live and horses gave him work he enjoyed.

He was blessed to be a part of a big family. John and Laura had a new baby. His brother, Bowie and Hart had built a bunkhouse just for their use. They called themselves bachelors. His mother and sister had a comfortable cabin together on the ranch. Of course, Jess and Mary Jane still had their home and a private cabin had recently been built for Pete. Blue John was offered one also, but he preferred living in the stables close to the horses.

All the cowboys and hands on the ranch made up the rest of the extended family. Some of them had forged careers out of working on the Triple B. With Pete as foreman, the ranch work was well-organized and managed.

He was so proud of the boys. Bowie and Hart were making names for themselves with the horses and cattle. Hart rightly gravitated toward Blue John for guidance and counsel and a link to his heritage. Marcus's brother had taken over the blacksmithing on the ranch. Many came from the community to have him shoe their horses and do other jobs for them as well.

Marcus could feel a strong magic pulsing through this place. A rhythm coursed through the air as if it was a living entity. It was so robust that it could be heard if one stopped to listen. There was a single heartbeat tying all the people together as one unit.

Curse whomever dared to try and break it them apart.

# ABOUT THE AUTHOR

Jana Dahmen was raised in West Texas herding cattle, stepping over rattlesnakes and drinking water from a cistern. She lived around cowboys who were of the real breed. She understands hardships dealt by nature and the energy required to clear hurdles. Thinking to leave those deprivations behind, she moved from Texas at the age of twenty.

She now lives in Wichita, KS in the middle of cowboy country. The home she shares with her artist husband and a Boston Terrier was built in 1890 and was originally the main house of a large ranch and farming spread. Though she no longer considers herself a cowgirl, her faith in Jesus, the values she lives by and how to be happy in a world wrought with chaos are rooted. Reflecting on her childhood experiences, she recalls not so much of the difficulties that seemed endless but more of the riches woven into the fabric of whom she has become.